PRAISE FOR ALL IN PIECES

"Brave, honest, and complex characters . . . will inspire
readers to see the beauty in broken things and give them the
courage to pick up the pieces and put them together again."

—Shaun David Hutchinson, author of *We Are the Ants*
and *At the Edge of the Universe*

"This book is full of raw, messy, beautiful heart."

—C. Desir, author of *Bleed Like Me*
and *Other Broken Things*

"*All in Pieces* is raw and real, and such a beautiful
story that I wish I had written it."

—Trish Doller, author of *Where the Stars Still Shine*

"A story that will touch your heart."

—Katie McGarry, author of *Walk the Edge*
and *Pushing the Limits*

"Young's characters are likable and believable in their flaws.
The protagonist's authentic voice makes this title
a fast read and hard to put down."

—*School Library Journal*

"Young is at her best when portraying Savannah's fierce love;
the bitter realization that she cannot protect or provide
for Evan is tremendously moving."

—*Booklist*

ALL IN PIECES

SUZANNE YOUNG

SIMON PULSE

NEW YORK   LONDON   TORONTO   SYDNEY   NEW DELHI

SIMON PULSE

An imprint of Simon & Schuster Children's Publishing Division
1230 Avenue of the Americas, New York, New York 10020
First Simon Pulse paperback edition November 2017
Text copyright © 2016 by Suzanne Young
Cover photographs copyright © 2016 by Jill Wachter
Also available in a Simon Pulse hardcover edition.
All rights reserved, including the right of reproduction in whole or in part in any form.
SIMON PULSE and colophon are registered trademarks of Simon & Schuster, Inc.
For information about special discounts for bulk purchases, please contact
Simon & Schuster Special Sales at 1-866-506-1949 or business@simonandschuster.com.
The Simon & Schuster Speakers Bureau can bring authors to your live event.
For more information or to book an event contact the Simon & Schuster Speakers
Bureau at 1-866-248-3049 or visit our website at www.simonspeakers.com.
Cover designed by Russell Gordon
Interior designed by Mike Rosamilia
The text of this book was set in Garamond BE.
Manufactured in the United States of America
2 4 6 8 10 9 7 5 3 1
The Library of Congress has cataloged the hardcover edition as follows:
Names: Young, Suzanne, author.
Title: All in pieces / Suzanne Young.
Description: Simon Pulse hardcover edition. | New York : Simon Pulse, 2016. |
Summary: "A girl struggles to take care of her younger brother with
special needs while confronting her own anger issues"—Provided by publisher.
Identifiers: LCCN 2016003832 | ISBN 9781481418836 (hc)
Subjects: | CYAC: Anger—Fiction. | Brothers and sisters—Fiction. |
People with disabilities—Fiction. | Bullying—Fiction. | Family problems—Fiction. |
BISAC: JUVENILE FICTION / Social Issues / Special Needs. | JUVENILE FICTION /
Social Issues / Bullying. | JUVENILE FICTION / Social Issues / Homelessness & Poverty.
Classification: LCC PZ7.Y887 Al 2016 | DDC [Fic]—dc23
LC record available at https://lccn.loc.gov/2016003832
ISBN 9781481418850 (eBook)
ISBN 9781481418843 (pbk)

FOR THE GIRL RUNNING
THROUGH THE BEAN FIELD AT NIGHT
WITHOUT A FLASHLIGHT

AND IN LOVING MEMORY
OF MY GRANDMOTHER
JOSEPHINE PARZYCH

CHAPTER ONE

My life is none of their business.

I don't want to be up here, don't want to explain my reasons, but I can't afford to miss another assignment.

I smooth my crumpled piece of notebook paper on the top of the podium. There's a cough in the back of the quiet classroom, and even my teacher looks bored as he sits in the faux leather chair he brought over from his last school—a school that could afford fake leather chairs, apparently. Mr. Jimenez is definitely slumming with us.

"My brother has an intellectual disability," I read, pausing once the words are out. I feel judged, exposed, and I look up at the class, anticipating a reaction. "He's not stupid," I add defensively. "He just learns differently." One guy curls his lip like he has no idea why I'm talking about this. A girl in the back pops her gum. The gravity of my confession is lost on them and it pisses me off. Pricks of anger crawl up my arms; anger at whom, I'm not sure. All of them, I guess.

I grow flustered and lose my place on my page, the already smudged ink going blurry. I look up accusingly.

"And if any of you even think of making a joke about him, I swear I'll—"

"What are you gonna do, Savvy?" Gris calls from the front row. He's leaned back in his seat with his long legs stretched under the desk, his immaculate Timberlands begging to be stomped on. "You gonna stab me like you did your boyfriend?"

I put my elbows on the top of the podium and lean forward, narrowing my eyes. "Give me your pencil, and we'll find out," I say.

Gris smiles, and the scar on his cheek is shiny under the fluorescent lights of the room. I sneer and rest back on my heels. Aaron Griswold is an alcoholic loser, and I'll tell him so the minute I'm finished. Just because we're both stuck in Brooks Academy doesn't mean we're friends. He isn't shit to me. But still, when he blows me a kiss a moment later, I nearly laugh.

"Enough," Mr. Jimenez calls from behind his desk. "Knock it off or I'll see you both after class. Savannah," he says to me, pushing his wire-rimmed glasses up on his nose. "Can you please continue?"

I'm not sure I want to—this is such an incredible waste of time. But I need this class to graduate, so I swipe a tangle of red hair behind my ear and begin again.

"Because of my brother's condition"—I lower my voice—"I picked a special-education teacher for my career project. The pay is terrible but the hours aren't bad. I think I'd be good at it. And I wouldn't be one of those condescending ones either. I'd be cool. I'd help the kids feel cool." I look out at the room of blank faces and sigh. "So, yeah. The end."

There's a halfhearted attempt at applause before Mr. Jimenez comes to stand next to me, barely two inches taller. He smells like copy machine ink and cough drops, and he's generally tolerant of our disinterest in learning.

"Thank you, Savannah," he mumbles, picking up the class roster.

I shrug and walk back to my seat, flipping off Gris before dropping down in my chair. As the heat begins to fade from my cheeks, I chip the clear polish off my fingernails.

"Nice speech, Sutton," Cameron says. He's in the desk next to mine, staring straight ahead and not looking at me. He never looks at me.

"Thanks."

"No problem."

I wish he never talked to me either. Things here at Brooks Academy are usually pretty simple. We show up and listen to the druggies, the criminals, and the anger management cases—like me—give speeches (or whatever pointless project is assigned), then we go home.

This is where the district sends the students they've expelled, keeping their funding by continuing our education. Yep. Glorified GED classes equal an education around here. But it's fine. I came to class and minded my own business.

Then Cameron Ramsey showed up, all sexy and quiet. None of us even know why he's in here. He definitely doesn't fit. I mean, the kid drives a BMW.

He's a distraction. And for some reason, I'm the only one privy to his one-liners. Nice speech? What the hell is that about?

"Cameron?" Mr. Jimenez calls from the front. "Would you like to participate?"

Cameron closes his notebook and shakes his head no. I wonder if he didn't do the assignment or if he just hates people. I understand either way. When the teacher moves on, Cameron takes out his phone and begins playing a game under his desk.

Mr. Jimenez leans on the podium, clearly exhausted. "Well, unless anyone else has something to add, I guess we're done for the day . . ." He leaves his offer open, but if he thinks any one of the twelve of us is going to prolong class, he's obviously having an acid flashback.

"Good-bye," Mr. Jimenez announces loudly and turns away. I feel sort of bad for the guy. He's youngish—young enough to still think he can make a difference in our lives. But he's our third savior this year. I wonder how many times a day he wishes he went into business management instead.

I stand and swipe my notebook into my bag, relieved the day is over. I turn just as Cameron shoves his phone into his pocket. Without looking at me, he smiles.

"I'll see you around, Sutton," he says.

"Uh . . . yeah," I respond. "Tomorrow. Here."

He laughs and starts walking away. "Right," he says. "That's what I meant."

I watch after him, confused, maybe blushing a little. Man. I don't know what it is about him. Okay, not true. I'll admit that part of it is his looks: chin-length blond hair, dark brown eyes, T-shirts that are tight enough to show off his muscles, but not the sort of tight that makes him look like a douchebag. But mostly it's because he talks to me. The fact that it's only me.

"God*damn*," Retha says, sliding up next to me. "Is Cameron getting hotter?" she asks seriously. "I think he is."

"He definitely is." We both stare toward the doorway, even though he's already gone. I glance sideways at Retha. "He talked to me again," I tell her, smiling.

"Of course he did. What did he say?"

"He told me 'nice speech.'"

She's impressed. I can see it in her eyes even through her gobs of black liner. "That's because he wants you," she says. "Now, can you please screw him and find out why he's here? I *need* to know."

"Sure. I'll get right on that for you." I swing my bag over my shoulder and survey the room. Travis is still asleep in the corner, his head down on his folded arms. "Grab your boyfriend," I tell Retha, motioning toward him. "I have to get home. Evan will be there in fifteen."

"Hey!" Retha yells toward Travis, making him jump awake. "Let's take off. Savvy's got her brother today."

Travis stares at us for a second, blinking heavily as if trying to figure out where he is. He straightens and brushes his long, black hair away from his face. "Okay," he says, sounding groggy. "But you drive, Retha. I think I'm still hungover."

"Well," I say as Travis strolls out the door with us, his skinny shoulders sharp under his thin, long-sleeved T-shirt. "That's what happens when you drink in the parking lot of a 7-Eleven until four in the morning."

"Hey." He smiles. "You could have been there too."

"Ah." I raise my finger at him. "But I don't drink. So I would just be tired. Not smelly and hungover."

His expression falters, and he lifts his arm to sniff.

"Gross, Travis," I say, pushing him hard enough to make him stumble. "That is seriously filthy."

Retha agrees and starts cussing at him in Spanish, making me laugh. I'm not bilingual, but thanks to her, I know every swear word. Hell, she even makes a few up as she goes.

"Relax, woman," Travis tells Retha, ready to play at fighting. But suddenly his expression hardens as he catches sight of something behind us in the hall. "Hey, I'll meet you guys at the car. I've got business to take care of." He touches Retha's arm as he moves past her.

I turn and see Gris leaving the classroom, hiking up his low-hanging jeans. Clueless as always.

"Travis," I say as he follows Gris down the hallway. Guess he hadn't been asleep the entire class after all.

"Let it go," Retha tells me, sounding bored. "Gris shouldn't have messed with you. He deserves the ass kicking."

She's probably right. Punches sometimes help—at least they help us. It's not like Travis is going to get in trouble. Gris knows better than to report it.

"Fine," I say, and start toward the parking lot with Retha. "But if I'm late getting home because of Gris, I will come back and stab him."

Hungover or not, Travis would never let anyone else drive his car. His Impala is old, and not in an "I'm restoring it" kind of way. It's rusted and the carpet smells lightly of mildew, but he keeps it clean like he's proud of it. Always swiping dust off the dashboard or sneaking into one of those do-it-yourself car washes when a person leaves before their time is up. So we're proud of it too.

We pull up in front of my house at the same time as my little brother's bus, and I know I'm too late. I grab my bag off the seat, yanking on the door handle. "I'll call you after," I tell Retha.

She raises her hand in a wave and leans over to adjust the radio volume. I slap Travis in the back of the head on my way out. He yells, but I'm already running toward the bus, my heart pounding. Evan is going to lose it.

I toss my bag onto the dirt of my front yard and stop outside the bus doors, panting as I wait for them to open. I can hear Evan crying through the open window. He likes to see me out here before the bus pulls up—he won't get off otherwise. Because if I'm not here, he'll think I left him. But I'm not Mom. And I'm not going to disappear like she did.

The doors screech open, and I climb up the steep stairs, nodding at the driver. She huffs out a hello, looking haggard. Exhausted.

I make my way down the aisle, and another little boy points to a seat across from him. I stop when I find Evan slouched down with his hands over his face. My heart breaks.

"Hey, buddy," I say. My seven-year-old brother hitches in a breath, still crying—but softer now that I'm here.

"You're late," he croaks in a small voice from behind his hands.

I swallow hard. "I know. Sorry."

Evan sniffles, still not showing his face. I hate myself.

"Let's go," I say, grabbing his backpack from the floor. "These other kids have to get home."

He's quiet and then mutters, "No."

"Evan," I warn, not wanting to get into it here. I wish I could just grab his arm and drag him off; it would be easier. But I don't put my hands on him like that. "Look," I say in a softer voice. "I'm sorry, okay? I fucked up. But if you come with me now, I'll make us dogs 'n' cheese. I promise."

"Really?" he asks quietly.

My lips flinch with a smile. "Yeah. But you'll have to help. You know how much I hate doing the dishes."

Evan finally drops his hands and looks up at me. His pale blond hair is wet where it's grown long near his eyes, and peanut butter from his school-provided lunch has crusted in the corners of his mouth.

He deserves better than me.

"Okay," he says. "I'll help you."

"We can even color," I tell him, taking his hand. I keep my voice light, trying to make it sound like there's something fun waiting for him inside our crappy house. There isn't. But I think he forgets that. It's like every day he starts new.

I wish I could do that.

It's too early for dinner, but I make Evan hot dogs mixed with mac 'n' cheese anyway. I don't ask him to help with the dishes, but he dries the plates. When we're done, we go into the living room and I give him his crayons and the backside of an assignment sheet I got at school.

Evan lies on his stomach across the worn carpet and spreads out his crayons in front of him. He draws a picture, occasionally looking up to make sure I'm still here. For a moment it's peaceful. Normal.

The front door opens, and my heart pounds faster.

My father's heavy boots clop through the hall until I feel his presence in the doorway behind me.

"Is there dinner?" he asks, his raspy voice shattering the contentment in the room.

"Yeah," I respond. "It's on the stove." I don't turn, hoping he'll get it for himself. Evan colors the sky purple.

"Come on, Savannah," my father says. "Can't you go plate it up for me? I just got home from work."

And I've gone to school, cooked dinner, and washed the dishes already, but I don't remind him of that. I lean closer to Evan and tap his paper. "Hey, buddy," I whisper. "Paint the house pink."

He looks up at me wide-eyed, as if a pink house is the most absurd thing he's ever heard. He laughs.

"No," he says. "The house is white."

"Yeah, but I want mine pink." I ruffle his hair and stand up. Evan reaches for the pink crayon.

My father stomps into the kitchen and pulls out his chair, scraping it along the scuffed linoleum floor. He exhales loudly, sounding tired. I understand the feeling.

I go to the stove and use the wooden spoon with the broken handle to stir the now-stiff macaroni before slapping a glob of it on a freshly washed plate. I set it on the table in front of my father.

He stares at the mac 'n' cheese with bits of hot dogs in it for a long moment before poking through it with his fork, looking disgusted. "Again?" he asks me.

I lean my hip against the sink and meet his eyes. "It's his favorite."

"Not mine."

I'd tell him that he's an adult and perfectly capable of fixing his own dinner, but I don't want to argue tonight. Not when Evan will be leaving soon. I look away, biting my lip.

We weren't always like this. When my mother was around, my dad would help her in the kitchen—hell, he'd even cook sometimes. He was never father of the year, but at least he wasn't useless. Now he can't make his own, let alone hold down a job.

There's a loud clank as he drops the fork on his plate. I turn and see him rub roughly at his face. "Grab me a beer, will you?" he asks.

"No. It's barely five."

He glances at me, looking sorry for a second. But he gets up and walks across the room to snatch a beer from the nearly empty fridge. He pops the top on his Bud Light the moment he sits back down at the table.

"Daddy," Evan yells, running into the kitchen. "Look what I made!"

Our father eyes him, taking a loud sip of his beer before answering. "Let's see what you've got there," he says quietly, holding out his hand.

Evan's jumping up and down, his energy out of place in this small, miserable kitchen.

"A pink house," our father says. I appreciate his attempt to sound interested.

"Uh-huh." Evan turns around to show it to me. "Savvy wanted hers pink."

I press my lips together and reach out to push his shoulder. "And see how good it looks?"

"Yeah." Evan laughs.

I look at our father and find him watching Evan with the same expression he always has when he's around him lately. A face of guilt, regret, resentment maybe—I'm not sure. But at least he knows enough to try to keep it to himself. He takes a long drink like he wishes he could drown himself in it.

"What color house do you want, Daddy?" Evan asks, stepping toward him.

"Doesn't matter," our father says. There's a pain in my gut when I see Evan's lower lip jut out.

"Make it a blue one," I answer quickly. "Daddy's favorite color is blue." I have no idea what my father's favorite color is, and I honestly don't give a shit. But I know Evan likes blue.

"Mine too!" my brother yells, flailing out his arms. He accidentally knocks into the can of beer and topples it over.

"Damn it!" our father snaps, pushing back in his seat as beer trickles off the table and onto his jeans. "What the hell, Savannah?" he screams at me, making Evan jump. "You're supposed to watch him!"

I ball my hands into fists.

"Come here, Evan," I say quickly, pulling my brother toward me. But it's too late. He's already begun to cry.

Hard. He hates loud noises, especially when they come from our dad.

"Oh great," our father says, raising his hands in the air, his lips pulled into a sneer. "Another fantastic night."

"Shut up," I say, hugging Evan to me. But my brother starts struggling, crumpling his picture into a ball and throwing it to the floor. "Stop," I whisper. But Evan digs his fingernails into my skin, and when I wince, he yanks free and runs toward the living room.

I swear and lift up the edge of my shirt to see the deep scratches along my side. They hurt, but I guess they'll go nicely with the bruise on my back from last week's tantrum.

The kitchen is quiet except for the sound of beer running off the table in a steady stream. I look over at my father and find him red-faced with anger.

"We can't keep doing this," he says.

"*You're* not doing anything," I answer. "I am."

"If your mother was here—"

"She's not. She left, remember?"

He narrows his eyes. "I remember, Savannah. I remember pretty goddamn clearly."

Does he? Does he remember what it was like the morning she left? Because I do. I was the one who called around looking for her. I was the one who had to miss school to babysit Evan. And I was the one who had to tell him that she wasn't coming back.

Evan was destroyed. I sure as hell remember that.

"This isn't working," my father says, motioning the way my brother had gone. "And it's not going to work." But there's a crack in his voice, maybe the last bit of his con-science wearing away.

"It's getting better," I say, knowing it's not true, but desper-ate to believe it.

My father blinks a few times as if clearing tears, and slowly moves to grab the dishrag hanging near the stove. "Just keep Evan out of my face tonight, Savannah," he whispers.

So I do. I walk into the living room and find my brother curled into a ball on the couch, most of his crayons broken on the carpet. He'd just gotten them back, too.

I close my eyes for a second, hating the moment. Hating my life. But then I straighten up, brush my hair away from my face, and get down on the floor to shove the crayons back into their box. Broken.

CHAPTER TWO

I have my brother mostly settled by the time our aunt arrives to pick him up an hour later. Once a week and then on weekends, our aunt Kathy takes Evan to her house, where she feeds him vegetables, washes his clothes, and reads him bedtimes stories. She won't be happy to know I already filled him with processed meats and cheeses, but it was the only way to get him in the house.

Tomorrow morning Kathy will personally drive Evan to school. But when the day is done, my brother comes back here, back to this. Back to me.

Kathy used to invite me along, before I was a dangerous felon. But I've been expelled from more than school. My mother's sister wrote me off. I'm not even welcome in my own family.

Travis's car is parked at the curb when I walk onto the porch. Evan and Kathy are already gone, and my father uses these nights as an excuse to get drunk. I prefer to be gone when he does that.

I let the screen door slam shut and jog down the stairs

toward the car. Retha leans her elbow out the open passenger window.

"Evan go with Kathy okay?" she asks.

"Yeah," I say. "She's got him this weekend, too. I should have told her no."

"She's a bitch." Retha's the type to hold a grudge. The minute my aunt stopped letting me in her house she went on Retha's shit list. In fact, the two can't be in the same room together without Retha cussing her out. But I like that about her—I like that Retha always has my back.

I get in the car and slide to the middle and lean between the front seats. When I do, I notice bruises on Travis's knuckles where he's resting his right hand on the steering wheel.

"That from Gris?" I ask him, motioning toward his hand. He didn't seem as banged up when he brought me home earlier.

"Naw," Travis says, flexing his fingers as he studies them. "I was working on the engine. Must have knocked it against something."

Retha glances at him, her brow furrowed. Travis's hangover should be gone by now, but you never know with Travis. He might be nursing a completely different bender at this point.

I nod and rest back in the seat. It's none of my business how he got those bruises. Retha turns away, and Travis shifts into gear before pulling his car out into the street.

I watch out the window as we drive. On my nights without Evan, I never know where I'll end up, and I never know when I'll be home. But it's nice. It's nice to be free for a little while. Even if it's not very often.

Our evening starts at 7-Eleven, just like it always does. Travis has his brother's ID, which is a direct violation of his parole, but it's not like we'd turn him in for it.

We park in our usual spot along the side of the building and Retha and I wait in the car as Travis makes the run. My beverage of choice is nonalcoholic. I watch my father get drunk all the time at home—I don't need to inherit his problem.

"I'm thinking of piercing my nose," Retha says, examining her face in the rearview mirror.

"You should," I agree. "Just don't let it get infected like your eyebrow."

She spins toward me and her black ringlets whip her cheek. "It was *not* infected!" she says.

"It looked disgusting."

"Shut up." She turns around. "Did I say shit when you pierced your belly button?"

"Uh, yeah. You called me a poseur."

She smiles. "You are a poseur."

I laugh and tell her to fuck off.

The driver's door opens, and Travis gets in, clutching a paper bag. He reaches inside and pulls out a soda.

"Dr Pepper," he announces, passing it back to me.

"Thank you."

"And for you, my love," he says to Retha, pulling out another bottle. "Mike's Hard Lemonade."

She leans over, her lips spreading into a smile. "Thank you, baby," she whispers, and kisses him.

I open my soda, letting it hiss so it doesn't bubble over. Just as I take a sip, Retha laughs.

"Holy shit, Savvy," she says, untangling herself from Travis. "Isn't that your boyfriend out there?"

My stomach drops, and I lower my drink. I don't have a boyfriend, but I do have a particularly psychotic ex. Then again, if Patrick were out there, Retha wouldn't be laughing. She'd be grabbing a bat.

"Who are you talking about?" I slide to the window and scan the parking lot, recognizing no one.

"He just went inside," she says. "Damn, girl. Is that a new Beamer?"

"Who?" I ask. "I don't know anyone with—" I stop when I realize she must be talking about Cameron Ramsey. I spot his car. "Same BMW," I say, even though I'm sure she already knew that.

"The new kid from class?" Travis asks.

Retha points a sharp fingernail toward the store. "That's him," she says. Retha turns to me and smiles. "Go say hi, Savvy."

"No." She's crazy if she thinks I will.

"Go."

"No, Retha," I say. "I'm not stalking Cameron into a 7-Eleven."

"Come on," she says like I'm just being stubborn. "The boy likes you. He talks to you."

"So?"

"He doesn't talk to anyone else," she says.

She has a point, and maybe he does sort of like me. Maybe. But it doesn't really matter. I'm still not following a dude from my delinquent class into a convenience store. I'm not a total loser.

"Let's just drive somewhere," I tell them, trying to sound like I don't care. But I can't help stealing another glance out my window. I look down at my soda, peeling the label for a distraction.

If it was a few years ago, maybe even last year, I could have tried for someone like Cameron. He might have fit in with my crowd—all the jocks and cheerleaders. But I'm not that girl now. And I don't have those friends anymore.

Besides, I don't have time for a guy to mess with my head. I have my brother to take care of. I'll always have him.

Retha leans over to whisper in Travis's ear, and I rest my head back against the seat. Travis starts the car and shifts into gear, but instead of driving to the street, he crosses the parking lot and parks next to the shiny black BMW.

I sit up straight. "Wait. What are you doing?" I ask him.

He catches my eyes in the mirror and shrugs.

"Traitor," I mutter.

"Time to pee," Retha calls, getting out. She opens the back door and ducks in to look at me. "You're coming with."

"Am not." There is no way.

"Get out of the car, Savannah," she says, "or I'm telling Cameron you're waiting out here to give him a blow job."

I burst out laughing. "You would never."

"She definitely would," Travis says. "I'd listen to the woman."

"No." I shake my head and turn back to her. "I'm calling your bluff, Retha. You would never embarrass yourself like that."

She bites her bottom lip for a second and looks me over.

"Okay." She slams the door and stomps toward the store.

I gasp. "Holy shit. She's not serious, right?" I ask Travis.

"I'd say she is."

"Stop her." I push his shoulder.

He laughs. "You know I can't stop Retha from doing anything. You'd have a better chance than me."

He's probably right, but I'm not going in there. I set my bottle in the middle console and lean between the seats, staring into the glass front of the store.

My heart speeds up a little when I see Cameron. He's carrying a bag of chips and a bottle of Mountain Dew, pausing at the cookies near the register. Retha walks straight toward him.

I watch as Retha talks to Cameron and he stares down at her, seemingly amused. He laughs once when she motions toward the car. He glances over and I duck behind Travis.

"This is such bullshit," I say. Travis snorts a laugh. I wait a moment, and when I peek in the store again, Cameron is staring at Retha, tilting his head as if confused. She continues to talk, and with his eyebrows hitched up, Cameron looks toward the car again.

He sees me, and his mouth flinches with a smile. No way. Does he actually believe her? Retha turns and waves at me, before taking Cameron's arm and leading him to the registers.

I'm going to die. How could she do this? She is seriously hard-core.

"Let's leave her," I tell Travis, knowing he'd never agree.

"You made your bed." He turns off the engine as if we'll be here for a while. He seems all too willing to participate in my humiliation.

The doors of the 7-Eleven open, and Retha and Cameron walk out. Cameron has a paper bag and a smirk on his face. I can't believe him. Is he some sort of pervert—thinking girls just give out blow jobs in the backseats of cars? Is that what he's into? I hope Travis kicks his ass.

Cameron opens my door, and I cross my arms over my chest and glare at him.

"Hey, Sutton," he says, looking down at the soda in my lap instead of at my face.

"Seriously?" I ask him. "I can't believe you'd even come out here. Are you really that desperate?" I can't believe I ever thought he was smooth.

Cameron furrows his brow and glances outside at Retha. She laughs and climbs in the front seat.

"Uh . . . sorry," Cameron says, turning back to me. He fumbles with the bag, reaching inside. "Your friend asked if I could buy this for you. She told me you were *dying* for one."

"Shit."

And then he pulls out a sucker from the bag. A lollipop. A Blow Pop to be exact. Cameron keeps his eyes on my sneakers and stretches the Blow Pop in my direction. My cheeks burn with complete mortification. I almost don't take the sucker, but having him stand outside the door like this is humiliating.

"Thanks," I say quietly, taking the Blow Pop from his hand. Now I feel sort of bad for calling him desperate.

Cameron straightens up. "Well, this was fun," he murmurs. "Have a good night." He closes the door and backs away.

Inside the car, none of us speak as we watch Cameron get

into his Beamer and drive off. When he's gone, Retha turns around, smiling wickedly. "Damn, he's fine."

"A Blow Pop?" I ask her.

"Better than a blow job, right? I mean, we don't just give it away, Savvy."

"You are so fucking evil."

"Aw, come on." She laughs. "It's okay to like him. How many guys would buy a girl a lollipop for no reason? Not many. He's a sweetheart."

"I'd buy you one," Travis says, sounding hurt.

Retha reaches over to play with his hair. "I know, baby," she says. "But we're past that stage of our relationship. Now I want things that are shiny."

They kiss, and I relax back into the seat, twirling the sucker between my fingers. Strawberry isn't my favorite flavor, but it still makes me smile. No one has ever given me a Blow Pop before.

Later, when Travis finally pulls up to my house at three a.m., I still have the sucker in my hand even though the stick has started to shred. Retha is passed out in the front seat, and Travis's eyelids are heavy. He raises his hand to me in a wave when I get out.

I wait at the curb as the taillights of his car disappear around the corner. Dread creeps in the minute I turn to look at my house. It's small with peeling white paint and a flat roof. The wide front stairs lost their finish a long time ago and are crumbling at the edges. No one will take care of it anytime soon. The house is pathetic. Like my life.

I sit on the top stair in the dark, facing the street. Over in the corner of the lawn (if you can call dirt a lawn) is a bumpy patch where there used to be a garden. It hurts to look at it, hurts to remember why it's there.

My family was almost normal before Evan. My mother even tried to plant a garden while she was pregnant with my brother. But after Evan was born, after she knew he wasn't going to be "right," she let the flowers die. Our family died with them.

I wipe hard at my face, pushing away the thoughts. The anger. In my other hand I clutch the Blow Pop. I bring it in front of me, staring at the white-and-pink wrapper. It's such a simple thing.

I think about Cameron, his face when I called him desperate. I should apologize to him, but I probably won't. I won't know how.

But I *am* grateful. And to prove it, I unwrap the lollipop and bring it to my lips.

CHAPTER THREE

I'm already so tired, but I'll have Evan after school today. My mornings are like this—filled with exhaustion, anxiety, maybe guilt. It hasn't always been this way. I used to be able to catch the bus with my friends. I used to have a life. I used to have a mother.

My alarm clock buzzes on the side table next to me and I slap it off. I roll onto my back and stare at the ceiling.

Gross. School.

Travis and Retha meet me out front with a cup of coffee and a Ho Ho. They are the best friends ever. They are also so hungover that they're moaning. It's a good thing I don't like alcohol. Spending half of my day nauseous sounds awful.

"You look terrible," I say to Travis when I catch his red-rimmed eyes in the mirror. "Should really stop drinking." I bite into my Ho Ho.

"Thanks, Mom," he answers, and turns up the radio. He always gets cranky when I bring up his drinking.

I've been with Travis and Retha for close to a year now.

Retha is like me—anger management issues. Only my weapon of choice was a number two pencil and hers was her fist. Travis has different problems altogether. Problems that keep him in and out of rehab.

"By the way," Retha says, turning to glance back at me, "I heard Lucinda Wilson is going to be starting at Brooks today. Keep that bitch away from me, all right?"

"I don't even know who she is."

"One of my ex-girlfriends," Travis says quietly. But Retha still turns to glare at him.

"Yeah," she adds, snaking her head. "And she'd better keep her nasty hands to herself or I'll break them off."

Travis sighs like he's tired of the conversation, and knowing Retha, this probably isn't the first time they've had it. Retha resorts to fighting before talking. She's all fists like that.

"I'll keep my eye out for a handsy ex," I say, sticking the last piece of Ho Ho in my mouth. "Just don't get me in a fight. Again."

Before I came to Brooks Academy I had only been in one fight—the one that sent me here. Even though, technically, it was "assault" and not a real fight. Now it seems like every weekend I'm running either to or from an ass kicking.

Retha smiles at me. "I'll try my best." As we walk into the classroom, Mr. Jimenez looks especially exhausted and clings to his podium, rustling through papers. The place is pretty much empty. But I do notice the shiny new blonde in the front row. Hello, Lucinda.

Travis makes a spectacle of wrapping his arms around Retha as he walks her to her seat. She and Lucinda exchange the required "bitch-ho" comments, and all is right with the world.

But when I sit down, I feel a little stab of disappointment. No Cameron. I'd been nervous to talk to him after the Blow Pop incident, but I was still looking forward to seeing him. I glance toward Retha just as she lies across her desk with a loud sigh. Travis retreats to his corner for a nap, and Gris is in his desk with his baseball cap pulled down to cover his black eye.

Mr. Jimenez straightens up at the podium. "Ah . . ." he says, looking over the class. "Fifty percent attendance rate. That's a new classroom high."

"High," Gris repeats with a laugh. Nobody joins him. We're all too tired.

Mr. Jimenez shakes his head in disappointment. "Okay. Let's get out our math workbooks and turn to page ninety-seven. I'll save the lecture."

Poor guy. I almost want to learn something just to give him a reason to live. Brooks Academy is like teacher purgatory—a world between college and a real gig. That is why most of the staff is made up of twenty-somethings with a save-the-world complex. But they all burn out eventually and it seems Mr. Jimenez is well on his way.

The class door opens, and Cameron walks in. I smile before I realize what I'm doing, and I stop before anyone can notice. Cameron has his blond hair pulled back tight and a crisp white T-shirt straining around his biceps. He watches the floor as he makes his way to his desk.

"Now we're really shooting for the stars," Mr. Jimenez says. "Even Cameron came to class today."

Cameron sits in the desk next to me, not acknowledging our teacher, and takes out a notebook. I watch him, but then I notice Lucinda leaning out of her seat to stare at him. I narrow my eyes at her until she turns around.

"Page ninety-seven?" Mr. Jimenez repeats for all of us.

Oh, right. Math.

I take out my workbook and flip through the completed pages until I notice Cameron staring down at his desk.

"Hey," I whisper. He looks sideways at me. "Math workbook."

Cameron slowly lifts his gaze, and when his eyes meet mine, it's like an electric shock to my system. My heart begins to race at the intimacy of it. He's looking at me, but more than that, I feel like he *sees* me.

"Thanks," Cameron says, and glances away quickly. I'm left a little breathless as he grabs his book out of his pack.

I hear a giggle from across the room, and turn to find Retha making an obscene gesture with her hand, maybe something to do with a Blow Pop.

"Retha?" Mr. Jimenez calls. "Not really appropriate."

She apologizes, and I cover my mouth as I laugh. Busted. I glance back at Travis, but he's passed out. Damn. No one to enjoy the moment with me.

I take out my pencil and begin scanning the math page. The questions are easy. Brooks Academy isn't college prep; it's barely remedial.

"How was the rest of your night, Sutton?"

I turn to Cameron. He's filling in math problems, talking toward his book.

"Good. Yours?"

"Good."

I blink, waiting to see if he'll go on, but he doesn't. He doesn't look at me again either. Suddenly lonely, I exhale, trying to pull my shit together and settle back against my chair to finish my classwork.

Evan's bus is late. I wait on the porch, looking up and down the street. Dread begins to fill my chest. This isn't good. It is never good when his bus is late.

I see the bus turn onto my street, and I jump up, relieved. But when it pulls to a stop in front of me, I know something is wrong.

The driver opens the door, and she hurries down the stairs to meet me outside. "I'm sorry, Savannah," she says quickly. "I couldn't get him to calm down."

My face grows hot, and I move past her to climb the steps. I go to where he was sitting the day before but find his seat empty. I can hear him. I hear his harsh breaths and whimpers as I move down the aisle. I find him curled up on the filthy floor under a seat.

The bus driver is next to me. "We were just down the street, and I'm supposed to call the school, but . . . I knew he just wanted you. I thought—"

"Thank you," I say, squatting down to reach out and brush Evan's hair.

I hear the boots of the bus driver as she walks away. I'm sure she's probably worried about getting fired—there are protocols she has to follow. But I'm glad she didn't follow them. Evan needs me. I need to be here for him.

"Hey, buddy," I whisper. He's shaking, and I have to swallow down my fear. "What happened?"

He sniffles. "They took it."

"Took what?"

"Your present. The boys took it."

I look to see if the driver has any idea what he is talking about. Because if someone fucked with my brother, I will go ballistic. The driver gives her head a shake, letting me know it wasn't like that. Evan . . . he gets upset sometimes. I don't blame him—kids can be dicks. But one small comment could equal disaster.

The bus driver nods toward the road, and I can see she's growing anxious. She has to get the other kids home. If I don't get my brother off the bus, she's going to have to call it in.

"Evan," I tell my brother seriously. "Get up now." I try to grab him by the arm.

"No," he screams, ripping away from me and banging my wrist into the metal bar below the seat. Vibration races up my bone, and I growl out my pain.

"Fuck," I curse, pulling back. Damn it. If I don't get him in the house, not only will the driver call the school, the school will then call my dad. They might even call my aunt. I can't give them another reason to take him from me.

"Evan," I repeat, keeping my voice low and controlled. A red mark with a blue center has already started to appear on my wrist bone. "Let's go."

"I don't want to."

He's not going to budge—at least, not in the next thirty

seconds. With tears pricking my eyes, I reach in and take him by the pant leg. I knot the loose-fitting denim and drag him out from under the seat, wincing as he kicks hard at my shin, but I don't let go.

"Leave me alone!" he screeches. The kids around us will probably be traumatized. Tell their moms about this terrible girl on the bus. The thought makes me sick. I hate making Evan this upset. I hate that I have to.

When I get my brother out into the aisle, I scoop his little body off the floor and lock his arms around him like a straitjacket, holding him close to me. Evan's screams fade into heavy sobs as the violence passes, and I back him toward the exit.

Another little boy grabs Evan's backpack and brings it to the driver. My brother is able to walk down the bus stairs on his own, clinging to my side. The driver follows us out and sets the worn backpack on the sidewalk in front of us.

"Thank you," I whisper, barely able to look at her. When I do, her expression tells me that this is the last time she'll do this for me.

My eyes itch with tears, and I turn away quickly to walk Evan into the house. I slam the front door behind us and lock it, and then lead him to the couch.

Evan climbs across the sofa and curls into a ball at one end, whimpering softly to himself. He's hurt and angry—confused, probably. I shouldn't have pulled him from under the seat. I should have just waited for him to calm down.

I sit on the arm of the couch and let myself breathe for a moment. My muscles are knotted up, and my wrist hurts.

My leg aches where Evan kicked me. It will bruise. It always bruises.

I turn to Evan and see that he's finally stopped crying. "So are you going to tell me what happened on the bus?" I ask him. "Why are you so upset?"

He opens his eyes and looks at me. "It wasn't on the bus," he snaps as if I'm purposely getting it wrong. I'm frustrated, impatient. Sore. But I try not to let him see that.

"Okay," I say, holding up my hands in surrender. "Then where?"

"At school," he says, sniffling hard. "I was waiting for the bus just like I'm supposed to. But the big kids came and took the present I made you."

My fists clench fiercely and I lower them to my sides. "What big kids? Where was your teacher?"

Evan shakes his head. "I don't know, Savvy," he whines. "I don't know where Miss Malloy was. But the boys called me stupid, and they took my backpack." His voice pitches up, starting to shake. "They dumped my stuff on the ground and they took your present." He starts to cry again. "It didn't belong to them. They shouldn't have took it."

"It's okay, Evan," I soothe, sliding down onto the couch cushion next to him. "Big boys are idiots most of the time. Besides, I don't need a present." My brother makes me gifts at least once a week. Anything from pictures to macaroni necklaces to bottle tops he glued to a frame. I'm running out of places around the house to put them.

Evan sniffles and looks up at me. "But I made it for you," he says. "You should get presents."

His blue eyes are red-rimmed and glassy. I lean my face close to his and kiss his nose. "Hey," I whisper. "I told you I don't give a shit about presents. You're my present."

The corners of his mouth twitch before they pull into a smile. I brush his too-long blond hair. "I'm a good present," he says.

"The best. Now, are you hungry?"

Evan nods that he is and wipes his face with the back of his shirtsleeve.

"Do you want to help or do you want to wait here?" I ask him.

"Wait here."

"Okay." I ruffle his hair and get up. I turn on the TV and adjust the antennae until the picture is mostly clear. I find a station with cartoons and smile at him. He smiles back.

I walk into the dingy kitchen and run the sink water until it gets hot and fill a pan to put on the stove. I turn it on to boil mac 'n' cheese.

And when that's done, I stand at the sink full of dirty dishes, cover my face, and cry.

CHAPTER FOUR

The night goes by too fast, and in the morning, I look across the classroom and find Retha leaning halfway over her desk, trying to get my attention. Her hair is tied into a high knot, her eye makeup heavier than usual.

I nod my chin, asking her what's up.

"Cut," she whispers loud enough for me to hear.

I snort a laugh, and next to me, Cameron grins at his notebook. Retha isn't exactly subtle. I check on Mr. Jimenez and see he's still writing line after line on the whiteboard. We're supposed to take down his notes, but some of us are making plans to cut class, apparently.

"I can't," I mouth to Retha.

"After lunch."

"No."

"Then get a ride home," she says out loud, obviously annoyed with me.

I widen my eyes at her. "You know I can't," I whisper harshly. "No money."

"Savannah?" Mr. Jimenez calls, startling me.

I turn to him, apologetic, and he gives me one of those teacher glares that says, "I'm really disappointed." Like I give a shit. "Sorry," I tell him anyway.

I slide my notebook in front of me and grab my pencil to actually start working. There's a chuckle from next to me, but I don't look. Being called out is embarrassing. I could kill Retha.

Travis and Retha bail after lunch, leaving me behind. I can't go with them—can't use up my absences. There'd been an incident at Evan's school earlier in the year where they needed me to come in. I'm allowed only ten absences at Brooks or they can fail me for attendance violation. And since repeating my senior year isn't an option, I stay.

When the bell rings at the end of the day, I get up and grab my things, anxiety rising up because I know I'll have to walk home. And I don't live close. Not even remotely close. Luckily, Evan has speech therapy after school, so I'll have an extra hour. I'll just walk fast.

"Hey, Sutton," Cameron says. I turn, surprised, and look at him.

"What?"

"You need a ride?" He's gathering his books, not watching me. Good thing because I gulp.

"No. I'm fine," I tell him.

"You sure?"

"Yeah."

He smiles and looks over, meeting my eyes. "I'm going that way," he offers.

"No, you're not," I say. "You don't even know where I live."

"Then how do you know I'm not going that way?"

He's finally looking at me, not flirting, just talking. But his dark brown eyes are unbelievably charming.

"Good luck, man," Gris calls to Cameron from across the room. "That one's got a violent temper." He laughs, brave now that Travis isn't here. I glare after him as he walks out the door. When he's gone, I turn back to Cameron.

"I'm good," I tell him. "But thanks anyway." I keep my head down because Gris made me feel stupid. Sure, I do have a violent temper—so says the court—but fuck Gris. He doesn't know me. He's about to get another black eye.

My hands shake and I press my books to my chest, not even waiting to put them in my backpack, as I start out the door.

What sucks is that I do need a ride. But I'm not just going to fall all over Cameron because he finally made eye contact. I have some self-respect.

I walk down the hall and push open the doors to the parking lot. The second I do, a wet breeze rushes in, smelling like earth and worms. It's absolutely pouring down rain outside. You have got to be kidding.

I set my backpack on the ground and shove my books inside. I don't have bus fare. I don't have anyone to call for a ride. So I zip up my pack and hold it over my head in a pathetic attempt to stay dry, and walk into the parking lot.

Immediately, fat splatters of rain soak my shirt and bleed into my sneakers. And it's cold. I get about halfway across the parking lot when a black BMW pulls next to me, keeping up. The passenger window rolls down.

"You sure you're sure?" Cameron calls. I glance over, and when I meet his eyes, both of us start laughing. I can only imagine how ridiculous I look right now. Still, I hesitate—even though I know it will take me half the afternoon to get home. There really is no other choice.

"Fine," I say, lowering my backpack and grabbing the shiny handle of his passenger door. I climb inside and stash my bag at my feet, rain dripping from my hair and clothes.

I look sideways at Cameron. "I'm ruining your interior," I say.

He shrugs. "It's just water." He lifts the corner of his mouth in a smile and flicks on the heater, sending a rush of warm air over my face.

He is so freaking smooth. And it's not normal. Normal guys don't just swoop in and offer me rides. Not without expecting something in return. I narrow my eyes at him, wanting to figure him out. Wanting to know his deal.

"Why do you talk to me all the time?"

"Do you not want me to?" he asks, furrowing his brow.

"You can or whatever. I'm just wondering why you talk to *me* and not someone else." His dark eyes are soul searching, kind. I pause in my bitchiness.

"Who else do you think I should talk to?" he asks.

"I don't know," I respond. "Talk to whoever you want. I just didn't know why it was me."

He turns away to look out the windshield. "Well, you do sit next to me. . . ."

Oh, great. He's going to be logical about it. "That's it?"

"Well, to be honest, you're not the type of girl I expected to find at the esteemed Brooks Academy."

"And what type is that?" I ask, unclear if he's complimenting or insulting me.

"Not really sure," he says. "Just not you."

He doesn't go on, and I feel slighted. "Why?" I ask. "What's wrong with me?"

He glances over, seeming surprised by my reaction. "No. Nothing. It's just . . . you've got this whole angry-girl-next-door thing going on. It's interesting."

What does that mean? How does he know I'm angry?

"Plus I dig red hair," he adds casually.

I stare at him.

"What?" he asks.

Of course. "Did you really think I was this easy?" I ask. "Are you some unbalanced asshole who tries to hit on vulnerable girls? I hate to tell you, Cameron. I'm not easily picked up. And I'm certainly not vulnerable."

"Who says I want to . . ." He pauses to laugh. "*Unbalanced asshole*? Really?"

"Oh, please. You 'dig red hair'? In my world that's a line. And a bad one, even."

"Yes, I said I like red hair. Not you, Sutton. Relax over there."

"Whatever." But his reaction seems genuinely puzzled. I may be projecting a bit—at least that's what the court-appointed therapist would have said.

Cameron puts his palm over his mouth and stares out the windshield as the rain comes down a little harder. I want him to start driving because this is really strange—the whole *me* sitting with *him* in a Beamer.

"Are you really going to take me home?" I ask finally. He smiles.

"I don't know. This is pretty fun. First time I've been called an asshole in weeks."

I laugh. "I find that hard to believe."

"But yeah," he says. "I'll take you home. Unless you want to go somewhere else first?"

"No. Home is good." But I wonder where he'd take me if I said yes. In fact, I'm surprised he'd be seen with me at all. He really isn't in the crowd I run with these days. He doesn't look like an ex-junkie or a fighter. He just looks . . . good.

Cameron switches on the windshield wipers. He waits a minute and I don't know if it's because he expects me to talk more. For someone who barely speaks, he sure likes to do it with me a lot.

"Sutton?" he asks. I look sideways at him, my heart speeding up.

"Yeah?"

"I sort of need to know where you live."

Right. I didn't think to tell him that. "Twenty-sixth and Division."

His mouth opens but he closes it quickly. I'm sure he doesn't spend much time in my part of town. He shifts his car into gear and begins to drive.

We're quiet for a while and he doesn't turn on his radio, which is really uncomfortable. I wonder what sort of music he listens to. I glance at his face.

Okay, seriously. Why is he taking me home? There's no way he finds me *that* interesting.

He notices me staring. "What now?" He smiles a little.

"Why are you taking me home?" I ask.

"Because it's raining. You were walking. I'd be a complete tool if I just drove by, right?"

"I'm used to tools."

He lets my words hang in the air, and I realize they make me sound bitter and scorned. Great. Of all the lines he leaves out there, it couldn't be one that makes me seem even halfway normal?

Cameron pulls onto Division and glances around the street. I'm glad it's raining. When it rains, people stay inside. He won't have to see my neighbors.

"Have you always lived out here?" he asks.

"Not really any of your business."

"Just making conversation."

"Yeah. I've always lived here." Although when my mother was around, the dishes were done and we ate more than mac 'n' cheese.

"Oh." He stares out the windshield, driving down my street, and each moment brings me more humiliation.

I motion to the houses. "You can stop here."

He slows down. "Which house is yours?"

"This is fine."

"Sutton, which house?" he insists, shaking his head.

Normally I wouldn't let a stranger know where I live, but I don't really have any fear of Cameron coming back. In fact, after this he might not waste his words on me anymore.

"The white one with the porch," I say, pointing across the street. I feel humiliated. I don't know where Cameron lives, but I'm sure it's nicer than here. He pulls to the curb and cuts the engine.

I'm surprised he turned off his car. "You can't come in," I say defensively. My dad would flip.

He smiles, staring at his steering wheel. "I didn't ask to."

I look out the window at my house, not wanting to get out, but knowing that I can't stay here. "What are you doing then?" I ask quietly.

"Talking."

"With me?"

"Obviously."

I fold my hands in my lap. It would be ungrateful to just walk off. I wait to see what he wants. I'm also a little curious.

"I've been wanting to ask you something," he says.

"Oh great."

"What's your deal with Blow Pops?" he asks. "Because you seemed pretty pissed when I brought you one. Wrong flavor?"

I laugh and tell him the story about Retha, leaving out any hints that she did it because I think he's hot. Without those details, she sounds like a real sociopath.

"I have to admit," Cameron says, chuckling. "That's hilarious. And if it makes you feel any better, I wouldn't have gone out to the car for a blow job. I do have standards. I mean, they're low. But I have them."

"That's good to know," I say.

Cameron exhales and leans his head on the seat, turning to look at me. "So how did you end up here?" he asks.

"Here?"

"In Brooks Academy."

"It's a long, tragic story," I say. "You?"

"I asked you first."

I resist the urge to answer with "I asked you second." Instead I say, "I got in a fight." Which is mostly true.

"Schools don't expel kids just for fighting," Cameron says. "Trust me."

"Mine did."

"No," he says, studying me. "Why did they really kick you out?"

I swallow hard, turning away from him. "Maybe I just left, and they didn't kick me out."

"Why'd they kick you out, Savannah?"

I look at him, startled by the sound of my name. It's strange hearing it from him. It's also exhilarating. He meets my eyes.

"What did you do?" he asks, softer.

"I stabbed someone with my pencil." It sounds like a lie. I wish it were.

"Why?"

He doesn't question it? Should I be offended? Do I look like someone who walks around stabbing people with pencils?

"He was a jock asshole," I say.

"Why'd you stab him?"

"What's with the twenty questions?" I ask, mocking his tone. I need to go. I shouldn't just be sitting in his car like this. I hardly know him.

"Because you don't seem the type that would go for jock assholes," he says. "So why'd you do it?"

There's a burn of shame in my chest, crawling its way up my throat. "Maybe I used to be," I say. "Besides, I told you it was a long, tragic story. One I don't feel like fucking reciting for you. How's that for why?"

Cameron grins at me. "You know you have some anger management issues?"

He catches me off guard, and I fight back my smile. "I've heard that once or twice."

"Me too," he says, and looks down.

Really? That seems unlikely. He's way too calm for that.

He turns to me. "Did you stab him because he was a jock asshole or was there a better reason?"

"Of course there was a better reason. He was my boy-friend."

"Huh. Remind me never to ask you out, then."

It's getting late. My father will get home soon and I shouldn't be out here with a boy when he does.

"Was that it?" Cameron asks. "Did he cheat on you or something?"

"No. That would have been easy."

I close my eyes. It's none of his business, but . . . I want to tell him. Goddamn it. I want him to know that I'm not just some delinquent. I had a reason. Nobody cared, but I had one.

"Well?" he asks.

I open my eyes and look at him. "He called my brother a

retard," I say, and it still hurts. It still digs into my soul. "In class, Patrick called Evan a retard, so I grabbed my pencil, and I rammed it through his hand. Thus, I was removed from the educational system."

Cameron's silent, and I immediately regret telling him. He thinks I'm a lunatic. I probably am.

"That's pretty intense," he says after a moment. I'm surprised by his reaction. He doesn't look nearly as freaked out as I'd expect.

"I'm guessing you didn't assault anyone?" I ask.

"Nope."

"What did you do?"

Cameron watches me and then starts his car. He nods toward my house. "Didn't you say you had to get home?"

Shut down. I feel betrayed, spilling my guts to him and not getting any guts in return. "You're not going to tell me?" I ask.

"I'm trying to stay mysterious. How else am I going to coax you back into my car?"

"You're not," I say. I grab the door handle, my heart racing, and pull my backpack from the floor. I climb out and jog through the rain toward my porch.

"See you at school, Sutton," Cameron calls from the driver's window.

I get to my door and turn to the car. "Go home," I yell back. Cameron smiles, unfazed by my attitude. He rolls up the window and drives away.

I stand there, watching until he's gone. And when he is, I smile to myself and walk inside.

CHAPTER FIVE

Cameron doesn't come to school the next day, which is just as well. I spent the night stressing over what I'd say to him now. I shouldn't have let him drive me home. Shouldn't have shown him where I live. I bet I stopped being interesting the moment he got back to the right side of town. Retha said she should cut school more often—maybe then I'd get some. I told her I was all set, but thanks.

Today's a Kathy day—at least it is now. She called shortly after I got home from school and asked if she could see Evan because it's her husband's birthday and they're having cake. I would have said no—it's not her turn and it means a long weekend, but I used up the last box of mac 'n' cheese and we have no other food.

I get my brother ready, and then I wait for Kathy on the front porch while Evan puts on his shoes in his bedroom.

Kathy shows up at exactly five and parks her minivan in the driveway. I watch her climb the porch steps. She's wearing a long, quilted coat with mittens on her hands like she's about to build a damn snowman with my brother.

It's not even that cold out, but her smile is decidedly chilly. Not cruel, but not sweet either. Like she's afraid I'll snap at any minute.

"Savannah," she says, nodding to me.

"Kathy," I reply, purposely leaving off the "Aunt" to hurt her feelings. I have a reason to be angry with her. It's not just about her turning her back on me. It's about Evan. Kathy thinks I'm a dangerous felon. That I'm untrustworthy, unfit. She wants to take my brother away from me.

Well, fuck her. She can't have him. He doesn't belong to her. I step aside to let her inside the house.

"Have you been going to school?" she asks, glancing over my clothes.

"I never miss a class," I answer, wanting to roll my eyes. Like she cares.

"That's good," she says. "Will you graduate?"

Of course I'm going to graduate. Just because I stabbed somebody, *once*, it doesn't make me a dumbass. "In June like everyone else," I say, maybe a little bitchy.

Her mouth opens for a second, but she closes it, ending the conversation. Kathy looks a lot like my mother, only older and more serious. It's another strike against her. She hasn't heard from my mom since she left, and she's given up asking if I've talked to her either.

Evan walks out from his bedroom and squeals when he sees our aunt. "Aunt Kathy!" He runs into her arms. I shift uneasily.

"Hi, honey," she says, hugging him and running her mitten over his hair.

I did my best to get Evan ready for her—his face is washed, and he's wearing the only shirt I could find without stains. Yet Kathy still looks at me as if I've left him in the wild to be raised by wolves.

She turns her gaze back to my brother. "How are you today?" she asks, smiling down at him.

"Good," he says, beaming under her attention. "But Savannah said there's no more macaroni and cheese."

"We'll fix you something nice," she tells him, and then looks up at me. "He really should be eating more vegetables."

"I'll let the chef know," I respond.

Kathy's expression hardens, but before she can dive into the benefits of green-leafy-shit-that-Evan-won't-eat, Evan squeezes Kathy around the waist, growing impatient. She starts to walk him toward the door, but stops abruptly like she forgot something.

"Oh," she says. "I made Evan an appointment at the dentist for Monday afternoon."

It's a shot to the gut. "But I can't," I say. "I'm in school."

"Savannah, he's never been to the dentist. He's seven."

It's an accusation, proof of my failure. "That's not true," I say defensively. "They check him at school every year."

Kathy's expression flips from annoyed to sympathetic, like I'm a kid who doesn't know any better. "They don't do X-rays there," she says, "and he needs a proper visit. It's important." She sighs, and Evan takes her keys from her hand and plays with the toys she's attached to them for his benefit.

"Look," she says to me. "I can take him. I'll pick him up

from school, go to the appointment—get him an ice cream after. Then I'll bring him back by six."

"Okay, fine," I say. "But he has to be back by six. He has homework."

"I can help him with his homework."

"No," I snap, but feel immediately apologetic when Evan looks up, alarmed by my tone. "No, that's my job."

"Savannah," Kathy says, taking a step closer to me and lowering her voice. "I'd like to take Evan one more day per week. We can make it long weekends or midweek—whatever's easiest for you. I know you're doing your best, but I think—"

I don't care what she thinks. She already gets Evan enough—nearly as much as I do. But before I can tell her no, she puts her hand on my arm.

"I'm not your mother," she says gently. "And I'm not trying to be." I yank away from her, not realizing how much that sentiment would hurt me. Kathy must see her effect, because she tucks her hands in the pockets of her coat.

"We'll use the extra day for Evan's speech therapy appointments," she says, as if it's a compromise. "Surely you see the benefit in that."

I wish her argument didn't make sense. But it does. I'm always late to Evan's appointments—it's hard to get across town on the bus, especially when I have to scrape together the funds for us. This would be good for Evan—I know that. But it still makes me feel threatened.

"Let's go, Aunt Kathy," Evan whines, growing bored of the key chain. I expect Kathy to scold him, but she's patient. It's painful to admit that she's more patient than I am.

"Savannah?" she says, waiting for my answer.

"I'll think about it," I tell her. She waits a beat, and then nods, probably reading that the answer is a reluctant yes.

She takes Evan's hand. "Say good-bye to Savannah."

"Bye!" Evan yells to me, waving wildly.

"Bye, buddy." I lean down and kiss his forehead. "Don't torture Old Aunt Kathy too much. She can't keep up with you like I can."

"Old," he repeats, then laughs.

"Good-bye," Kathy says cordially, and heads toward the door.

I don't say anything back. I watch as she holds my little brother's hand and walks out of our house and into her waiting minivan. Evan likes her, so their closeness shouldn't hurt me as much as it does. She is family, and Evan needs someone like her in his life. Someone mature and patient. Someone who can make a dentist appointment. But there's no way she loves him like I do.

I wave from the porch so that Evan can see me, and when they're gone I exhale heavily—worried, but also partly relieved that he'll eat well tonight.

When my father gets home just after dark, I spend forty minutes trying to convince him to give me money for groceries. He stands at the kitchen sink, washing engine grease from his hands. He shuts off the water and shakes his palms dry before popping the top on his beer.

"How do I know you're really going to buy food?" he asks.

"Because who else gets the food around here?" I ask, disgusted. "Not you."

Not really me, either. Most of it comes from the food bank. Retha's mom picks me up a bag once a week when she goes, but Evan's been eating more lately. He's growing so fast.

I work when I can and use the money for food, but because I take care of Evan, my available hours are limited. None of the places keep me on beyond a few weeks.

My father drinks from his beer, watching me, distrusting me. "You going to buy alcohol?" he asks.

I scoff. "No."

"Drugs?"

"Don't be stupid." He's pissing me off. "Look, do you want to eat or not?" I ask him. "There's nothing here—not even mac 'n' cheese. So if you want to go grocery shopping, have fun. Just bring back food."

My father sets his can on the counter and scratches his head. His reddish brown hair has gotten long. It looks dirty, unwashed. "I don't want to go," he says after a pause.

"Well?" I ask. "Then I need money to shop with."

He sighs, annoyed. Like I'm the problem. Like everything is my fault. Or Evan's. My dad pulls his wallet from the back pocket of his grease-stained jeans and opens the billfold. He gives me forty dollars. I forget to thank him, and walk out to call for a ride.

I'm relieved the minute I get out of my house and into Travis's car. The smell of his car is more familiar than the scent of my own house. More comfortable, too. I'm beginning to have trouble remembering what my father was like before he was a drunk. Before my mother left us. When

I'm with my friends, we don't have to talk about it because they get it.

"Hey," Retha says, looking back at me from the front seat. "I have to go to the mall first, and then we'll go to the grocery store."

"Come on," I whine. "I hate the mall."

"Don't care." Retha adjusts the radio, turning it up loud enough to drown out my voice. I reach between the seats to turn it down and appeal to Travis.

"Don't do this to me," I tell him.

He shakes his head. "Sorry, Savvy. I've already been out-voted."

"Technically, that's not possible," I say.

"It is with Retha. Besides, I'm just the driver. I'll meet up with you later. I hate the mall."

"Bastard."

He chuckles.

Mall shopping sucks, especially without money. I'm not sure what Travis had to barter to get out of this, but he drops us off at the entrance. I follow Retha into the mall and she drags me to five different stores where I wait for her to try on clothes. It's basically hell.

When I was in middle school I used to hang out at the mall. My family never had extra money, but we had enough to get by. My father was at least working steadily then. My friends and I would eat pizza and watch cute boys. It was so superficial and stupid. I pause, realizing that I can't even remember what it felt like then, free from responsibility. So much has changed.

Retha grabs the sleeve of my hoodie and yanks me forward.

"Hurry up," she says. "Travis is meeting us in the food court in like ten minutes, and I want to go to Old Navy."

"I can't," I say, untangling my shirt from her grasp. "You're killing me. Why don't you go get the jeans, and I'll wait with Travis?" I nod like this is the best idea in the world.

She stops dead and turns to me. "You know I need you to tell me how my ass looks. How am I supposed to get jeans without a second ass opinion? Mirrors lie."

"Oh, please. You know you look fantastic in everything you wear. Now, meet me in front of Subway."

"You suck," she says. "Tell Travis to get me a turkey sub." She turns away and starts down the hall.

I make my way toward the bright lights and overwhelming smells of the food court. Subway is the only decent restaurant left. The pizza place shut down, and the Wok Shop lets their food sit out from open to close.

I scan the large area and find a ton of empty tables, but no Travis. I locate a spot near the fountain that's out of the way but not out of sight, so he and Retha will be able to find me.

I sit and fold my hands on the table. My stomach growls with hunger. I haven't eaten since breakfast, and that was a half-crushed cupcake that Retha gave me.

Hopefully Travis will buy me dinner. I don't have any money to spend; I never do. All I have is the cash for groceries and that's for Evan.

I glance around the food court and watch as people feed their kids french fries, toss away nearly full plates of food, or try to use chopsticks unsuccessfully.

Within minutes I'm bored out of my mind and I'm starting to stress about Travis. Whenever he's late, it's either because he fell asleep or he got high. He better be asleep.

"Hey, *Slut*ton," a voice calls loudly.

My heart seizes, and a mix of humiliation and anger crawls over my skin. I keep my head down, but I have to give my ex-boyfriend credit for coming up with *Slut*ton. I didn't think he was that clever.

"Hey," he says louder, as if the problem is that I didn't hear him the first time. Several people turn to stare. A mother looks concerned. Aw, hell. I turn around.

"Fuck off, Patrick," I say in a low voice.

He glares at me from next to the fountain. He's exactly the same: short brown hair and icy blue eyes. Patrick's cute enough to make him popular, because that way, people don't try to look too deep inside. And he's rotten.

Luckily he's also alone. The last thing I need is a bunch of ex-friends *and* an ex-boyfriend harassing me.

"Now, is that nice?" Patrick asks, his mouth pulled into a sneer.

"Nicer than you deserve. Yes."

He clenches his oversize jaw and slides his hands into the pockets of his khakis. I wonder if he's trying to cover up the scar from where I stabbed him.

"How's juvey?" he asks, coming over to sit across from me. My mouth opens, surprised, but I try to cover it quickly. I haven't been this close to him since I was dragged out of class in handcuffs.

I straighten my back. "It's an extended learning center,

jackass. And it's fantastic. I don't have to deal with assholes all day."

Patrick smiles to himself, looking down at the table—like I'm being funny. I can't believe we ever went out. The first guy to call me beautiful and I waste half my junior year on him. I was an idiot. I should have been able to see past his bullshit.

"So they're going to let you graduate?" he asks, looking up at me. "You should be in jail."

I chew on the inside of my lip. The way he's watching, as if I'm a piece of meat, makes me cringe. His gaze pauses at my boobs and then at my mouth. I fold my arms over my chest, and he seems to revel in the power my discomfort gives him.

"What do you want?" I ask. "Why can't you just leave me alone?" My pulse races—he once told me he'd kill me for what I did. His harassing phone calls may have stopped a few months ago, but he's obviously still angry.

Patrick sets his hands on the table, stretching them out to rest in front of me as he leans in close. I recognize the smell of his cologne, and it makes me a little nostalgic. But then I remember how much I hate him. My eyes drift to the scar on his hand. It's still pretty gnarly.

"You know you've never apologized?" he says almost sweetly. I lift my eyes to meet his. They're pale blue; I used to like that about him.

"Yeah," I respond. "I know."

He waits. Well, he can wait all day—I'll never apologize. Patrick treated me like shit our entire relationship. He put me down, made me feel like I should be lucky to have him because of where I came from. And then the day I tried to break it off, he blamed Evan.

"Savvy?" Travis's voice is immediate comfort. I look up as he walks toward me, jetting a concerned glance at Patrick. Travis's long hair is tangled and wild, like he just woke up. I smile, relieved to see him.

"Great," my ex-boyfriend says. "Another one of your new degenerate friends?"

"Go to hell," I say, braver now that I'm not alone.

Patrick reaches out and grabs my hand from across the table. It's a movement so sudden and forceful, I lose my breath. He yanks my arm toward him, dragging me onto the table.

"I should put a spike through your fucking hand," he hisses in my face.

"Hey!" Travis yells, running over to pull me free.

But I'm shaken, gasping. I didn't expect that. I should have expected that. Patrick's been asking me to apologize since he came to my court appearance, but I sort of thought he'd be over it by now. When the calls stopped, I thought he would too.

Travis grabs Patrick by his polo shirt, hauling him out of the chair and pushing him into the aisle between the tables. "Don't you ever put your hands on her!" Travis shouts. Around us everyone stares.

I can barely breathe as I look between Travis, my skinny, ex-drug-addict friend, and Patrick, a linebacker. I'm still shaking. He grabbed me. Patrick grabbed me and pulled me over the table. This is some next-level shit.

Patrick laughs, brushing off his shirt as if Travis's touch dirtied it. As if Travis is dirt. Patrick glances at me and raises his chin, confident. Powerful. "I'll be seeing you around, *Slut*ton," he calls to me. And then he turns and walks out the mall exit.

I try to calm down, look normal and unfazed. It's near impossible to fake. I sit back down in my seat, and Travis joins me at the table, taking the spot where Patrick had been.

He studies me for a moment and then leans in. "You okay?" he asks.

I nod, but no. I'm not. I'm freaking out. Patrick has gotten under my skin again. He's rattled my confidence.

"Let me see your wrist," Travis asks quietly, holding out his hand. I glance at his arm, the sleeves of his shirt pushed up to the elbows. On his skin are the leftovers of needle tracks not yet faded. He sees me looking.

"They're healing," he says, meeting my eyes.

I press my lips into a smile and look for fresh holes. "Almost gone," I say, wishing it were true. But it has only been three months since the last time Travis shot up. And two months before that. They'll never truly be gone. So I'll never stop checking for them.

He lowers his eyes, and I give him my hand. As soon as he takes it, I see the handprint Patrick left across my wrist.

"Jesus," Travis says, turning it over. "He really grabbed you."

"Yeah."

"Sorry I was late."

I sniff a laugh. "It's okay," I tell him. "You didn't know it was Psycho Day at the mall."

Travis smiles and sets my hand gently on the table. He feels sorry for me. Everyone always feels sorry for me, if they feel anything at all.

"Where's Retha?" he asks, looking around.

"Shopping for perfect-ass jeans."

"Ah. Good," he says with a laugh. He nods toward the sub shop. "I'm guessing she wants turkey?"

"Yep."

"On it," he says, standing up. "You hungry?"

A slap of guilt hits me, and I stammer out a response. "I mean, if you don't mind," I tell him. "I'll pay you back."

"Shut up, Savvy," he says, waving me off. "You don't owe me anything."

And I appreciate him saying that. Sometimes I feel like he and Retha are the only people who don't want anything from me. They don't keep a tab.

He walks off, and when he's gone, I pull my hand into my lap, rubbing absently at my aching wrist—like I can wipe away my vulnerability. And I wait for something to eat.

I carry the groceries inside the house, my sleeves pulled down to cover the bruise on my wrist. Not that my father would ask—he never asks about my bruises. He stares at me as I walk in, and I pause in the doorway and look at him.

"What?" I ask. He's not fully drunk yet, so I can still talk to him. But since Evan's not here, I know it won't be for long.

"You get groceries?" he asks.

I hold up the bags.

He looks down at the floor, and I know that's not the real question. My shoulders tense, and I lower the bags to my side.

"How long are you going to do this?" he asks in a low voice.

"Do what?" But I know what he's talking about. He's constantly saying that Evan is too much for me to handle. That I'm not enough.

"Kathy wants Evan to live with her."

My hands begin to tremble. She already gets him an extra day a week. I'm not about to let her take him away from me entirely. "No," I say.

"She has the means—"

"He doesn't need money," I say quickly, glaring at my father. "I take care of him."

"You're seventeen."

"You're forty. What's your excuse?"

My father's jaw clenches, and I know I shouldn't challenge him now. But he knows I'll fight. Evan is his son—he should fight for him too. Just because my mother couldn't handle it, doesn't mean that I can't. I'm stronger than her. I love Evan more. And I'll never leave him. I'll die first.

"It's too hard," my father says. He almost looks guilty.

"He's ours," I whisper forcefully. "And he's not going anywhere." I stomp toward the kitchen.

"It's not really up to you," he says under his breath.

I fight back my tears and set the grocery bags on the counter. I look out the window into the backyard. The weeds have overgrown the lawn, and the patio is covered in moss and dirt. There are no toys. No swing set. I hate this life.

But I love Evan and I will never give him up. Not without a fight.

CHAPTER SIX

Nearly the entire class is absent on Friday. Only ones here are me, Gris, the new girl, and Travis. Retha had to babysit her baby brother so her mom could go to the DMV. She told me to send her regards to Mr. Jimenez.

It's quiet—worksheet day since a lecture would be a waste of air on Mr. Jimenez's part. I steal glances at the door, hoping Cameron will walk in. But he never does. Travis sleeps his way through the morning, but still manages to turn something in at the end of the day. Neither of us mentions the incident at the food court again. I don't like the reminder of what helpless feels like.

"Retha told me that you're going to her house?" Travis asks after class, holding open the door to the parking lot for me.

"Yeah, I guess," I say. "Evan's with my aunt through the weekend. Don't really want to be home."

"I get it," Travis says, running his hand through his long hair. He looks tired. Maybe even miserable.

"You're coming too, right?" I ask.

"Naw," he says. "Not tonight."

I climb in the passenger side of his car and look over at him. "Everything okay?"

He gives me a small smile, one that tells me to mind my own business. I respect his privacy, and I figure it's between him and Retha.

Travis stops at Retha's house, and she comes outside like she's been waiting for us. Travis waves at her, but Retha purses her lips and sets her hands on her hips.

"Yikes," I say under my breath.

"I'll catch you later," Travis says, switching the car into gear. I scrunch up my nose, feeling bad for him even though I don't know what their fight is about. I say good-bye and climb out of the car.

I meet Retha on her porch, and we watch Travis drive away. When he's gone, I look sideways at her.

"I see things are going well."

"Oh, girl." She shakes her head, and then yanks open the screen door. "Don't even get me started on him." She goes inside the house, but I take another look at the empty street, feeling torn, like a kid whose parents are fighting in front of her.

"Savvy," Retha's mother calls in her thick accent as I close the door.

"Hi," I say, walking into the kitchen to give her a quick hug. I tower over her small frame, and we both look at the table when Retha's little brother wails from his high chair. "Hi to you, too, Raymond," I say, wiggling my fingers at him. He smiles and drools all over himself.

I love coming here. Retha's house smells like cooking oil

and spices. Her dad is always working, but when he's here, his booming laugh is just like Retha's.

This entire place is loud and messy. It's like a home.

"So how's Evan?" Retha's mother asks, stirring a pot of soup on the stove. "You haven't brought him in a while."

"He's with our aunt this weekend. I'll bring him over next week."

"You got enough to eat there?" she asks, tapping the wooden spoon on the side of the pot with a clank. "I'm going by the food bank next week."

"We're okay," I say, even though we never have enough. But I hate asking her to help us with groceries. She has her own family to take care of. She shouldn't have to take care of mine, too.

She pats my hip. "I'll bring it by on Tuesday."

I smile and thank her. Retha stops at the kitchen table and spoons yellow baby food into her brother's mouth, wiping away what he spits out. She kisses the top of his head, and then tells me she has to get ready.

I follow her to her room, saying hi to her little sisters, who are piled on the couch watching cartoons. Retha closes her bedroom door, and I turn to her.

"Your mom doesn't have to get us food," I say, slightly embarrassed.

"She likes to help," Retha says. "Don't be stupid about it."

"Not trying to be; I'm grateful. I didn't even have enough for hot dogs this week," I admit.

"That's because your dad is an asshole," Retha says, shaking her head. "I'll pick up some hot dogs and drop them by." She stops at her dresser and positions a compact on the edge to use as a mirror. She picks up her eyeliner and swirls it around her left eye. Before lining the other, she spins to face me.

"Did Travis tell you why we're fighting?" she asks.

"No. He probably figured you'd want to be first."

"Or he knows enough to be ashamed."

"I don't think I want to hear about it," I say. Their fights are rarely one-sided—they're usually both at fault. I lean back in the cushions of the bed, pulling a small stuffed alligator from under my thigh.

Retha's bedroom cracks me up. She shares it with her two little sisters, but the amount of pillows and stuffed animals in here is ridiculous. Her cousin works for a company that fixes those claw games, so Retha's an expert. She can get you anything you want on the first try.

I whip the alligator at her leg.

"Ow, bitch," she says, making me laugh.

"Fine," I say, knowing that my lack of curiosity is what's really annoying her. "What did Travis do now?"

She smiles. She would have told me whether I wanted to know or not. "Remember Casey?" she asks.

"Casey the girl or Casey the guy?"

"Travis's girlfriend in middle school. The one with those dumbass pink streaks in her hair."

"Did she used to be a cheerleader?"

"Yeah."

"Ugh," I say. "I hate that girl." And I sort of do. Once upon a time, when I cared about things, she kissed one of my boyfriends and talked shit to me. It's been a long time since I've had problems that simple.

"I hate her too," Retha says. She doesn't hate every girl—she's not shallow like that. But when you don't have much, you hold on to what matters. You hold on with both hands. "Anyway," Retha continues, "Casey called Travis last night."

My eyes widen and I sit up. "*What*? Not cool."

"Right?" Retha turns back around to ring her other eye with liner. "You know she still likes him."

"Is that why she called him?"

"I don't know." Retha snaps the compact shut and leans against the dresser, folding her arms across her chest. "Travis won't tell me."

"What do you mean?" I ask her. Travis is a good guy—he doesn't do drama for drama's sake. No, when he messes up, it's big-time. Like shooting heroin or breaking into cars. Not cheating on his girlfriend. That's petty.

"He told me she called," Retha says, her eyes growing teary despite her hard expression. "But then he said that it wasn't a big deal and that I needed to get over it."

"Get over it?" I nearly shout, climbing to my knees. Telling your girl to *get over it* without explaining yourself is almost an admission of guilt.

"Yeah," Retha says like she can't believe it either. "He said I would overreact. But what the fuck? Obviously something shady went down. What if they're hooking up?"

I'm in shock. Travis and Retha are special together. Sure, they fight a lot, but they love each other. No one's allowed to ruin that.

"So what are you going to do?" I ask, my fingers trembling with adrenaline. I know what she wants and it will probably involve hair pulling. I'm sick of getting into fights with Retha, but at the same time, it's the weekend. There's always a fight somewhere.

"It's Friday," she says. "Everyone from Kennedy goes to the cornfield, right?"

"They sure do."

"Good. So I think maybe we should stop by. Hang out a little."

Her lips curve into a devilish smile. Retha doesn't want to hang out with those pricks. I'm the one who used to hang out with them, back when I thought I could. Back when I was part of a family, dating the future homecoming king, thinking I was normal.

But what is normal anyway? Taking care of Evan is my normal. This is who I am.

"Hello?" Retha yells, tossing a lacy black thong from her drawer at me. It bounces off my chest and I sweep it away with a laugh. "Are you game or not?" she asks.

"Depends," I tell her, trying to hide the sudden panic I feel at seeing my old classmates. "Do you think Patrick will be there?" I sound weak. I hate it.

Retha's expression softens. She knows what happened with Patrick at the mall, but like Travis, she doesn't bring it up. "If he's there," she says slowly, "I'll knee him so hard in the balls, he'll never have kids."

"That would be a good thing."

"Definitely."

We stare at each other a moment, an acknowledgment of fear without the words. Then Retha rubs her lips together to smooth her lipstick and checks her reflection one last time. But my heart is still racing—I haven't seen anyone from Kennedy since I was expelled. What will they say when they see me? What will they do?

I can't be scared of them, though. I can't *let* them scare me. I begin to twist my hair around my finger, glancing out Retha's bedroom window at the sky. This is a bad idea.

"You want to borrow something to wear?" Retha asks, startling me.

"No, thanks." My clothes are faded, a little old and oversize. But I hate borrowing things.

"Come on, Savvy," she says. "I'll even let you wear *The Shirt*." She grins.

Damn. *The Shirt.* Retha has this one fitted shirt that whenever I wear it, no shit, I hook up. It hugs me just right and makes my boobs look fantastic, or maybe it's just a random coincidence. Either way, whenever I wear it, I get lucky. Every time.

And I wouldn't mind a kiss.

"This sucks so hard right now," I mumble as we make our way through the crowds of freshmen in the darkened field. We're not far outside the city, barely in the suburbs, but one farmer used to have functioning cornfields here. He retired, but the corn still grows on his land. Now the locals have carved out a path and use it to party.

"I swear we were never this desperate as underclassmen," I say, looking sideways at Retha.

"Hell no," she agrees. "They're nasty."

We've already been hit on three times and nearly groped by the "key master." It takes Retha two tries to convince him there are no car keys in her pocket. The second try ended with a heel to his shin. He should have known better than to try exploring her jeans on his own.

I keep my head down, my hair falling forward to cover my face. I hope no one will recognize me—especially since the last image they have of me was when I was getting carried out of school, calling Patrick a son of a bitch with his blood on my shirt. This is a really bad place for me to be.

"Savannah Sutton?" someone calls. My heart nearly stops.

I look over slowly and find Spencer Harris. He's a running back and a friend of Patrick's. We'd gone to school together since kindergarten, but he looks at me now like I'm a piece of shit. I used to think he was a nice guy.

Retha stops, looking at him and then me. "You need help?" she asks quietly.

I shake my head no and wait as Spencer approaches. Retha takes a step back. I like that she doesn't force the issue—she knows I can handle myself.

"Wow," Spencer says, looking me over. "I thought you were in jail."

"Nope." Once upon a time, Spencer and I were friends. I'd been friends with a lot of people. But after I got arrested, they all forgot that. They all chose Patrick's side, even though they knew he was an asshole. But it wasn't like they were going to turn on one of their own.

Retha looks away, watching the party. Spencer moves

closer to me and nods his chin toward her. "These the sort of people you hang out with now?"

I clench my jaw.

He laughs. "Real classy."

"Fuck you, Spencer."

He reaches out and clasps my shoulder, massaging it, but squeezing until it hurts. I begin to shrink back. "Be nice," Spencer tells me through his professionally straightened smile. "I forgive you for screwing up my boy. And you know," he adds, glancing down my shirt, "I still think you're really hot. Even if you are psychotic."

"Homicidal," I growl. "Now let go." His fingers are digging deep into my muscle, but I refuse to let him know how much he's hurting me.

Spencer fake gasps as if I offended him. "That's not very friendly, Savannah. How about . . ." He looks over his shoulder toward the high rows of corn. "How about we go out there, and you can make it up to me?"

Sickness swirls as I stare at him, wishing I had a pencil to drive through his face. I don't, so I'll have to settle for a knee to the sack.

"There she is," Retha calls, walking over and grabbing me by the arm. She pulls me out of Spencer's grasp and points toward the keg. I crack my neck, sliding my hand over hers where it rests on my arm, and we walk quickly. My fingers tremble.

"On the way out," Retha says, fluffing her black curls for the benefit of people staring at us, "I'm ramming my fist through that asshole's teeth for putting his filthy hands on you. And if I find a weapon . . ."

I smile, squeezing her hand. "He keeps a baseball bat in the back of his truck."

"Done."

I rub my shoulder, trying to loosen the muscle, and Retha points toward the keg again. It takes a second, but I find the girl with dumbass pink stripes in her hair. Casey is talking and laughing with some guy I recognize from my time at Kennedy. Her hair is teased, her lipstick is dark brown, and she wears ridiculously long fake eyelashes on her wide-set eyes. She might even be wearing glitter. She's like a child who got into her trashy mom's makeup.

Retha and I exchange a glance. "Ready?" she asks me.

My earlier moment with Spencer has thrown me off, but I say yes anyway. This is part of my gig as Retha's best friend. Sometimes we have to argue, fight. That's all there is to it. When people think you're a delinquent, they treat you badly, they disrespect you (like Spencer). This is the only way to get that respect back. Even if that respect is motivated by their fear.

Casually, Retha and I make our way toward the keg. A couple of people call out to me, mostly saying what's up or asking how I am. I guess not everyone hates me. But I don't acknowledge them. I barely remember them.

When we stop at the metal keg, Casey doesn't look up at us. She's smoking a cigarette and laughing as she talks to the guy. Retha grabs a blue cup out of its plastic sleeve and begins filling it with beer from the keg, glaring at Casey. The girl doesn't even notice. How can she not feel Retha's stare? It's like a million daggers tipped with poison.

As soon as the cup is full, Retha brings it to her lips and

takes a long sip. Then she pulls back her arm and tosses the entire cup of beer at Casey's face. There is a *swoosh*, followed by the *clink* of the plastic cup hitting the dirt, and a shrill scream. She sure felt that.

"What the hell?" Casey calls in a high dolphin pitch.

I laugh. She looks ridiculous. Her mascara is running down her cheeks, and Retha's beer soaked only half of her head. The other side of her hair is still perfectly styled.

"You call Travis?" Retha asks. She sounds calm. Eerie, scary calm.

The guy next to Casey is staring between her and Retha, holding back a laugh. I can tell he's hoping for a girl fight, as if it would have anything to do with him. Creep.

Casey's face tightens as she realizes just who Retha is. She must recall that Retha is not only Travis's girlfriend; she's also the girl who punched Mrs. Crowe in the face. Casey narrows her eyes.

"It's none of your business," she tells Retha, tossing her wet cigarette in the dirt at Retha's feet. The guy next to Casey takes a step back, his lips forming a perfect O.

"Just tell me," Retha says. "Did you call Travis?" Again with the eerie calm.

"Yes," Casey replies. "I did."

"What did you say to him?"

Casey laughs. I can't believe she's challenging Retha. "I told you it's none of your business," Casey says, waving her head from side to side. Her mascara is nearly to her chin before she swipes her cheeks to clear it. Then she flicks the wetness off her fingers.

"What did you say to him?"

This is about to get ugly. I glance around the party. This isn't our typical crowd—these kids tell the cops everything. I notice several people watching, but we're not a spectacle yet. We'll have time to run. The 7-Eleven is only a few blocks, and we can call Travis for a ride from there.

Casey smirks and sets her beer cup on the side of the keg. "Fine," she says. "You really want to know? I asked Travis if he was done slumming with his Mexican whore."

My mouth falls open, and behind Casey, the guy laughs.

"Excuse me?" Retha asks, and her accent seems to thicken. "I'm from Puerto Rico, bitch!"

Casey has obviously lost her mind, talking to Retha like that. But then I see her side glance, and I follow her gaze. Damn.

Casey's looking at a couple of girls, big ones, who are on their way over to jump us from behind. One of them has a large stick in her hand.

I exhale and roll my shoulders. Guess she's not as stupid as she looks. She's a fighter too. Well, here we go.

Without a word, I swing out my arm and punch Casey right in the eye. She flies back off her feet and I feel an immediate vibration shoot up my arm. I hit her pretty damn hard. She's on her ass, screaming.

"Run!" I yell to Retha, and grab her hand. We start for the field, and I glance back and see the two big girls take off after us. We might get our asses beat tonight after all.

"You knocked that bitch out," Retha says with a loud laugh as we push our way through the corn, people yelling behind us.

"She had backup," I say between gasps. "We were about to get jumped."

Stalks of corn whip my arms, and I know I'll be covered in scratches, but my adrenaline keeps me numb and pain free. I had no choice. If I hadn't hit Casey, her friends would have beat us down right there. At least the hit was a distraction to get us out of there. But hell, my knuckles hurt.

"They're getting closer," Retha says.

"Take a left," I tell her, and cut that way, knowing the street is just beyond the rows.

"They're heading for the road," one of the girls behind us calls out.

They're going to catch us. I curse and run faster.

Retha is at my heels as we break through the rows and onto a deserted road. Getting beat down on concrete is no fun—I've been there before with Retha. Not too long ago either. In fact, I have a scar on my chin.

Heaving in breaths, Retha points to the other side of the street. "7-Eleven?" she asks, half bent over.

"Never make it," I say back. My lungs burn, like they might explode.

"Never say never," Retha calls, and bolts.

I groan and run after her. Soon the voices behind us start to drift away. They might have gotten turned around in the corn, or they might just not have the stamina to chase us this far. Rich girls aren't used to running for their lives. We are.

By the time we get to the 7-Eleven parking lot, I need to die. But I need a drink more.

"Let's see if they'll give us water," I gasp, leaning over to rest my palms on my knees. I wait a moment, and then straighten. As we walk through the sliding door into the shop, the bright lights amplify every scrape and scratch. Stupid corn.

The woman behind the register eyes us suspiciously as we stagger in, probably looking like a couple of drunks as we head for the soda fountain.

"Can we have water?" I ask the cashier, taking the smallest cup and holding it out.

"Fifty cents."

"For water?" I ask. Is she kidding?

"Hey, Sutton."

My stomach flips and I slowly turn. Cameron Ramsey. While my hair is plastered to my head with sweat, dirt and blood coating my arms, Cameron looks perfect. He's wearing a button-down shirt with khakis turned up at the ankle, no socks. His hair is tucked behind his ears, and even from here, I can smell the light scent of his cologne. Retha's right—he is getting hotter.

"Fancy seeing you here," I tell him. "Do you live at the 7-Eleven?"

He chuckles. "Do you?"

"Okay. Good point."

"I was dropping a friend at home. Stopped to get refreshments." He holds up a bottle of Coke. "What are you doing out here?"

"Uh . . ."

"Hi, Cameron," Retha says, saving the moment. She lifts her hand in a wave. "Will you buy us a couple of sodas?"

I turn and glare at her. I can't believe she would just ask him to buy us something. This girl has no filter.

"Sure," Cameron says. When I turn to him, he looks at me and smiles. "No Blow Pop though, right?"

I fight back my laugh and shake my head no. Luckily, Retha doesn't hear him, and he doesn't tell her that he knows the truth. It's like our little secret.

"What do you want to drink?" he asks me, grabbing two large cups from the holder.

"Nothing," I say, and slip my hands into my pockets. I see Retha wander down an aisle.

"Really?" Cameron asks me. "Not even a water? You sure?"

"Yeah."

"But you're sweating."

I'm also dying of humiliation. "No, really. I'm fine."

He shrugs. "Okay."

Damn. I'm thirsty. But I don't want to owe him anything. Well, anything else. He's already given me a lollipop and a ride. What's next?

Retha appears again with a bag of chips. "Cameron," she says, like she's known him all of her life. "Can I use your phone real quick?" She brushes her black curls from her face. "I need to see if Travis can pick us up."

Cameron looks over his shoulder from where he's at the soda machine, filling up a cup with Dr Pepper.

"Sure, but do you guys need a ride somewhere?" he asks. He finds the tops for the sodas and presses one on. With his back to us, Retha glances at me and smiles.

I widen my eyes at her and mouth "no."

"Actually," she says sweetly to Cameron, licking her lips suggestively even though he can't see her. "We'd love a ride. That is sooo nice of you to offer."

"Retha," I say as warning. She laughs.

"Cool," Cameron responds, and turns around, oblivious to our struggle. Retha straightens quickly like she's a saint. "Let's do it," Cameron adds, making Retha crack a smile.

He grabs another drink and fills it, but he doesn't look at me again, doesn't ask if I'm really sure I don't want one. He laughs with Retha instead, handing her a drink. It's stupid, but I'm a little jealous. I liked it when I was the only one he talked to.

I hang back as he walks around with Retha, letting her pick out other snacks she wants. Again, he doesn't ask me. When they're done with their shopping spree, Retha and I go out front to wait next to the Beamer while Cameron pays for it all.

"I can't believe you," I say to her, totally pissed. Another ride home, another conversation. Opening up my world to someone like Cameron is a bad fucking idea. I can feel it. And besides, I'm embarrassed that he knows I can't even afford a cup of water, and yet, here's Retha asking him to buy her Slim Jims.

"He wants to screw you," Retha says as if it makes it all fine.

"He does not."

"*So* does."

"Maybe he likes *you*," I tell her. "You're the one always asking him to buy shit."

She laughs. "Don't be bitter. Oh, wait," she says, "I know what it is."

I look sideways at her. "What?"

"*The Shirt.*"

We stare at each other for a second, and then we both break out laughing. She's totally right. That damn shirt. It has to be more than a coincidence.

Just then a car pulls into the parking lot. It takes me a second, since I'm still smiling, thinking about *The Shirt*. Then I hear, "There they are!"

"Oh my God," I say, grabbing Retha. I'm about to run when the door opens and Cameron comes out of the store, holding a bag while balancing two sodas against his chest. He looks at us.

"You could have stayed to help me carry stuff," he says.

"Get in," I yell to both him and Retha.

Retha opens the back door and dives in, while I quickly round the car and get in the passenger seat. Cameron follows but pauses outside his door, unable to open it with his full hands.

I lean over and pull the handle, stretching across the seats to push it open for him. He catches it with his elbow, and I straighten to see the Honda full of bitches racing through the parking lot toward us.

"Move your ass, Cameron!" I shout, reaching to grab the bag from his hand and shoving it on the floor at my feet. He laughs, climbing in, and looks at me like I'm insane.

But I'm actually kind of scared. "Please," I tell him, trying to sound calmer. "I'm about to get jumped."

His face falls, and without asking for further explanation, he sets the sodas in the cup holders and slams the door. He starts his car and slips his arm behind my seat, turning to back us up.

The girls stop their car on the side of the convenience store and get out, running toward us and shouting. Only now they have two more girls.

"Run them over," Retha says, leaning up between the seats.

Cameron stifles a laugh and turns the wheel sharply, heading in the other direction.

Chasing after us, Casey stops to take off her boot. She chucks it at the car, bouncing it off the hood. But Cameron drives fast, and soon they're just standing behind us in the parking lot, flipping us off.

"She threw her fucking boot?" Retha says, grabbing a soda and sitting back in the seat like this is a normal car ride. "She's pathetic."

Cameron is pressing his lips together so hard I think he might hurt himself.

"Something funny?" I ask him, just realizing that I'm riding shotgun and wishing I had dived into the back with Retha.

"Not at all," Cameron says seriously. "I'm used to people throwing their shoes at my car." He looks at me, and I smile. Okay, I can see how that might be a little humorous to him.

He nods down at the cup holder. "Got you a Dr Pepper," he says as if I'd asked for it specifically. I look down at the drink, and then turn toward the window, my face warm. His kindness is too easy. I worry about the strings that are attaching to me.

"Cameron," Retha says between slurps from her straw, "you should have seen Savvy tonight. She knocked a bitch out."

He turns, seeming surprised. "Really?" he asks me.

"No. She wasn't knocked out," I murmur. I don't want to brag about fighting. It isn't something I'm proud of—yeah, there's a rush at first. But that's always followed by guilt. Even when the person deserves it.

I glance sideways at Cameron and find him looking at my hand; my knuckles are red, soon to be a pretty shade of purple.

"She may not have been unconscious," Retha says, "but did you see her swollen eye in the parking lot? Shoot. She'd better invest in some dark sunglasses."

"Shut up, Retha." I rest my elbow on the window and lean my head into my palm. To be honest, my hand hurts, and my throat burns from running. But I still don't want to take that soda.

"Wow," Cameron says. "Sounds like a fun Friday night. Remind me not to take you to any parties unless I have a getaway car waiting."

"Go to hell," I tell him.

"Don't worry, Cameron," Retha says, biting her straw. "I'm sure Savvy would be a perfect angel with you."

I spin to look at her but she just winks. She's dead to me.

"Oh," Retha says to Cameron, finding his eyes in the rearview mirror. "Can you drop me off first? I need to tell Travis his girl got beat down."

She's leaving me alone with Cameron now? Not just dead

to me—dead. I'm going to murder her later. I lean my head back against the seat.

Cameron listens as Retha gives him directions, and when we pull up in front of Travis's house, I begin to shake my leg with nervousness. I don't even know what to talk to Cameron about. I already told him about my expulsion. I don't want to give him any more details.

"Thanks," Retha calls to him. "You really saved our asses back there."

Cameron nods and waves to her.

"Call me," Retha sings at me as she climbs out. The door closes and I can feel Cameron watching me. I don't look at him.

"You know," I say, my head lowered, "I'm only a few blocks away. I can just get out here."

"And end my night?" he asks. "Thought we were having fun." I turn to him, and he smiles, highlighting how miserable I seem. In truth, I'm not. "You can get out," he says, "but I'd like to take you home."

My breath catches, and I have no idea what to say.

"You know," he goes on, "in case anyone else plans to hit you with their shoe."

I laugh, and although it's awkward, I nod and tell him that it's probably safer that way. He shifts into gear, and even though I didn't ask him for the soda, I quietly take it and sip from it anyway.

"Thank you," I whisper. He doesn't respond, which makes me feel less like a beggar.

Cameron stops in front of my house; I'm surprised he

remembers which one it is. But then again, he's probably never been to a neighborhood like mine. I'm sure most of the people he knows live where houses have lawns.

"Thanks for the ride," I tell him, grabbing the handle of the car door.

"Thanks for the excitement."

I laugh, and he looks over at me like he knows me. And for a moment I wonder if he does. If somehow he knows that I'm not as fine as I seem. I wait a moment longer than I should, holding his gaze. And then, as if it's the only response, I lean over and kiss his cheek.

Before I can think about how unbelievably stupid I am, I get out and jog toward the house, my face on fire. That was so dumb.

I push heavily on my front door, and before I slam it shut, I hear, "You looked nice tonight, Sutton. We should go out more often."

Damn *The Shirt*.

CHAPTER SEVEN

When Travis picks me up on Monday morning, he looks terrible. The rings under his eyes are dark and his hair is uncombed. Retha stares out the passenger window, actively ignoring him. The entire weekend has gone this way, and at first I thought it was about Casey. But now I'm not so sure. This seems more serious.

"Hey, Savvy," Travis mumbles.

"Hey." I look cautiously between the two of them. The car smells like beer and I crinkle my nose. "Damn, Travis," I say, sitting back. "It reeks in here. You'd better hope the cops don't pull you over."

"He'd better hope his parole officer doesn't find out how much he's been getting wasted," Retha hisses, not looking at us.

I meet Travis's eyes in the mirror, expecting him to give me a "she's exaggerating" look. But instead he turns away.

He's hungover. Again. There's a sinking feeling in the pit of my stomach. My father's an alcoholic too, but I refuse to sympathize with him since it comes at the expense of me and my brother. But Travis . . . He grew up with a dad who beat him up, one who dislocated his shoulder when he was five. One who still beats the fuck out of him every time he gets paroled. I know why Travis drinks. And I know why he shoots drugs in his arm.

I just wish I knew how to help him stop. But I'm not a counselor. Travis will stop when he wants to, and nothing Retha or I can do will change that. No matter how much we want to.

"We're just dropping you off, Savvy," Retha says from the front seat. "We're taking a ride out to Cleveland today."

"For what?" I ask. Even if I did want to skip with them, I wouldn't go on a day like this. On a day when they hate each other.

Retha glances at Travis and then turns to me. "His dad's up for parole," Retha says quietly. "Travis has to appear at the hearing."

"Oh." My heart sinks. Travis's dad is the worst of the worst. No wonder Travis is so messed up right now. Retha's going with him to make sure he doesn't get high while he's there. It wouldn't be the first time.

The reality of the moment is harsh, and I stare into my lap until we get to school.

When I walk into the classroom, I see Mr. Jimenez standing at the front with his glasses on the podium and rubbing his eyes. Yeah, I don't blame him. Eight a.m. is definitely too early to socialize.

The bruises on my knuckles have faded to a less dramatic blue, but the scratches on my arms have turned to thin scabs.

I'm not feeling my best. And the fact that Travis and Retha aren't here makes me feel all the more vulnerable.

Cameron is texting at his desk. His hair hangs loose and when he brushes it behind his ear, I roll my eyes at how effortlessly good-looking he is. I almost say hello, but I chicken out and sit down to wait for the bell.

"Morning," Cameron says as his thumbs slide over the keys. He doesn't look over, but I know he's talking to me.

"Hey," I respond, completely self-conscious. I let down my guard on Friday; I even kissed his cheek. I'm not sure if I want him to acknowledge that or not. I mean, I guess not. That would be awkward. But then again, if he's already forgotten me or if it wasn't a big deal . . . I stop myself. I'm seriously overthinking this.

Cameron's phone buzzes in his hand, and he laughs as he reads the text. He types out another message. I wonder if he's talking to a girl, and there's a small stab of jealousy in my chest. Weekends can be long if you're having fun. He might have met someone. Or, hell. He might have already had someone.

I take out my notebook and set it on my desk, staring at the front of the class and wishing Mr. Jimenez would start teaching. I hate the silence right now. It makes me think too much. I tap my pencil on the cover of my notebook.

"You nervous about something?" Cameron asks.

"No."

"Why are you tapping, then?"

I stop and fold my hands on my desk.

"Your friends not coming to class today?" Cameron asks.

He's still on his phone. God—why won't he look at me? He must think I'm pathetic—getting in fights and asking for rides home.

"No," I tell him. "They're not."

"Too bad."

"Whatever," I mumble. I'm surprised by how much his texting irritates me.

"Whatever?" he repeats and turns to me. He sounds amused.

I don't answer. Mr. Jimenez exhales loudly from the front, and I pretend to be interested in what he has to say instead.

"All right," Mr. Jimenez says. "I know I promised to lecture today, but we're going to do some writing and cut our day short at twelve. Anyone have a problem with that?"

"Got a hot date, man?" Gris calls, chuckling at his own joke.

"No, Aaron," Mr. Jimenez responds. "I have jury duty and there are no subs available."

"Jury duty?" Gris asks. "Anyone we know?"

And I have to laugh at that one. Because it's quite possible that one of us would know them. It's not that big of a town.

"Not sure. But I'll keep you updated," Mr. Jimenez says sarcastically. "Now, anyone else have an objection?"

The class is silent because who in their right mind would refuse a shortened day of school? Although for me, leaving early isn't necessarily a great thing. Not only do I not have a ride home; I'll have more time to spend there. Evan's bus won't arrive until three and Retha and Travis won't be back until tomorrow.

"Hey, Sutton?"

I turn sideways to Cameron. He looks dead at me, and I forget why I'm even annoyed with him.

"What?" I ask.

"Want to go to lunch?"

My heart begins to race. "With you?"

He tilts his head. "Yeah. I don't have anyone to go to lunch with. Want to come with me?"

"No." I do.

"Please?" he asks.

"I can't."

"I'll buy."

I'm about to get pissed at him for being a condescending asshole when I realize that he's not. People with money do stuff like this: offer to buy each other lunch as a bribe to hang out.

I turn and stare down at my desk. "I'll think about it," I tell him.

"All right."

So I think about it. Obsess, really. Over the next four hours, I dream of all the places Cameron will take me and I think of all the reasons I can't go. So when Mr. Jimenez finally tells us to head out, I'm well prepared with a "Sorry, I can't" speech.

Cameron stands up and stretches, his T-shirt lifting high enough to flash the skin above his belt. I run my eyes over him, enjoying the view. He laughs to himself, and I realize he caught me checking him out.

"So what'd you decide?" he asks as if he knows the answer.

"I can't go," I tell him seriously.

His expression falters and I think he's disappointed, but I might be imagining that, because he grabs his notebook and raises his hand in a wave before walking away. There's a dull ache in my chest. And my stomach growls.

I gather my things and move slowly out of the classroom. It's a lonely walk to the parking lot. I hate how stubborn I am—he was going to buy me lunch, not take me on a date. Nondating is okay. Why do I have to be such an idiot all the time?

I push through the double exit doors and survey the parking lot. I wish I had bus money. I curse under my breath and start walking in the direction of my house.

A black Beamer pulls up next to me.

"The thing is," Cameron says out his window, as if we're in midconversation, "I just thought since your friends aren't here, that maybe you'd want to keep me company so I don't feel like a loser sitting by myself at McDonald's."

I stop walking and stare at him. He eases his car next to me. I want to go with him.

"Come on," he says, smiling, even as his eyes study mine. "I'll buy you a Happy Meal."

I laugh.

"Is that a yes?"

"A maybe," I tell him.

He waits, holding my gaze, and I feel all sorts of unrealistic feelings for him. The dangerous kind that would complicate my life. I slide my hair behind my ear.

"I'm really hungry," Cameron says. "In fact, I'll be eating too much to talk."

"Now you're tempting me," I say. "McDonald's?"

"Unless you have someplace better in mind?"

"No," I say. "I think that would be fine."

"Well, great. Then get in before I gnaw my arm off."

I debate a moment longer, afraid to start something with him that I can't finish. I don't want to get hurt. But logic fails me, and I get in anyway.

There's a McDonald's near the school, but I ask him to drive to the one closer to my house. One within walking distance.

We go inside, and the restaurant is a bit dingier than the other location, definitely not one of those McCafés. But it does have a playground. Before my life fell to pieces, my mother would take us here to play.

Cameron does indeed get me a Happy Meal, and we find a clean booth near the back. The minute Cameron sits down and opens his box of Quarter Pounder, I tilt my head and look him over.

"So why are you at Brooks?" I ask him. "What did you do?"

He smiles. "Who says I did anything?"

That's the thing with troublemakers—we cling to that innocent-until-proven-guilty bullshit. Even so, I can't begin to guess what Cameron is really doing there.

"Kids with Beamers don't go to Brooks Academy," I tell him.

"I do."

"Why, asshole?" I laugh. "Quit acting so secretive."

Cameron widens his eyes. "Me? You're calling *me* secretive, Miss I-don't-want-to-get-dropped-off-at-my-house?"

"You're stalling."

"You're right."

I wait, actually admiring the fact that he doesn't want to talk about himself. Too many people these days want to talk about themselves all the time. You don't see me and Retha running around trying to explain ourselves. If people misunderstand, well, that's on them.

Cameron takes a sip from his Coke, drawing out the silence. He looks around the restaurant, probably hoping for a distraction, but the place isn't distraction worthy. Old people and five-year-olds are hardly enough to provide entertainment.

"Fine," Cameron says, as if I've dragged it out of him. "I trashed a school."

I straighten up. "You did?"

He swirls a fry in ketchup. "Yep."

"Bad?"

"Hundred thousand."

I gasp and lean forward. "How the hell did you cause a hundred thousand dollars in damage?" I ask loudly.

Cameron chuckles and looks around the room, his cheeks reddening. A couple of the senior citizens are staring at us.

"Can you keep your voice down, Savannah?" he whispers, acting offended. "This is a family restaurant."

Again, the use of my first name is a bit of a shock. "Sorry," I say.

But I'm fascinated. Is Cameron actually some anger management head case like me? Is that why he talked to me in the first place?

Cameron eats his fry, chewing slowly. He doesn't look like he plans on elaborating, but if he thinks he's going to get away with not telling me about his crime, he's crazy.

I kick his sneaker under the table. "How did you ruin that much stuff?"

He sucks in his lower lip, and when he releases it slowly, I feel the flutters of attraction. Is he purposely trying to side-track me?

"Nice try," I say. "Now tell me."

He shakes his head like he's embarrassed he got caught trying to charm himself out of this conversation. "Okay," he says. "I flooded part of the building, broke some computers. A few windows. Some appliances." He scratches his head. "Maybe the trophy case."

"That's pretty badass," I say. "Did you get arrested?"

"Yep. You?"

"Yep."

"Bet our parents are proud," he says.

I laugh and pick up my last chicken nugget. I take a bite, and Cameron looks between me and my empty tray.

"Do you want more to eat?" he asks.

"No." I'm still hungry. I'm always hungry.

Cameron nods and wipes his hands on his napkin. I finish chewing, letting the silence fall over us. It isn't uncomfortable. I'm glad he's not the kind of person who feels he has to fill the silence. They were like that at my old school—afraid of being boring, and instead they became boring by talking all the time.

I play with the straw in my drink, moving around the ice cubes. "Why'd you do it?" I ask, truly curious. It seems so out of character—well, out of what little character I know of him. "Were you failing or something?"

He winces. "Why? Do I look dumb?"

"Sort of." But I know he's not. He may not participate in class, but I've seen him whip through his quizzes. I've seen the As.

"Oh, thanks." Cameron settles back in his seat. We're both done eating, but I don't want to leave yet. I don't want to go home.

"What was it, then?" I ask.

"Apparently I have bad friends."

"That's not a good enough excuse," I tell him. "Because I had 'good' friends and I still put a sharpened number two through Patrick's hand."

Cameron presses his lips together, looking at the table. "What can I say, Sutton? I'm weak-willed?"

I smile. "Counselor diagnosis?"

"Yep. And the judge."

"Nice."

"And you? Anger management?"

"Uh-huh."

"I can see that," he says. "Although I think you've been managing pretty well since I've known you. I mean, other than that time you punched a girl in a cornfield. But I'm sure you had a reason."

The fact that Retha and I went there to fight probably negates any reason I had to punch Casey, but I don't tell Cameron that part. "Technically," I say, twirling my straw, "you still don't know me."

"Right." Cameron nods. "We should change that."

He quickly looks away, the dine-and-dash of flirting. He

seems well versed, and I have the sudden awful feeling that I'm being played.

"So, do you take all of your girlfriends to McDonald's for lunch?" I ask.

"Girlfriends?" He grins. "Plural, even."

I shrug. "I'm sure you've got a few."

"Are you trying to ask me out, Sutton?"

"No," I say. "I'm just wondering if this is part of your game."

"My game?" He's laughing at me. "No," he says, moving his tray over to lean his elbows on the table. "I do not take girls to McDonald's to impress them. I was hungry."

I look down. I shouldn't have brought it up—shouldn't have shown that it bothered me.

"And just in case you're wondering," he tells me, "no, I don't have a girlfriend." He says it offhandedly, but I can feel him waiting for me to look up.

"Good for you," I say.

"Do you have a boyfriend I should be watching out for?"

I glance at him. "Why?"

"Don't you think he'd be jealous that I'm charming the hell out of you right here in your local McDonald's?"

"Oh, were you being charming?"

He stares at me, looking pleased, sort of devious. His brown eyes are deep and it's a good thing he doesn't look at me very often because they're filled with electricity. I'd never finish my classwork.

"Do you have a boyfriend?" he asks again, more seriously.

My face begins to tingle, almost like he's asking me out

even if he's not saying those words. And I don't want him to. "No," I say. "I don't have a boyfriend. I stabbed the last one."

He nods, not giving away his feelings on the matter. Then he slaps his palm on the table, startling me. "Well, glad that's out of the way," he says. "I should go. Let me bring you home."

I've already let him bring me to lunch and buy it; I can't get back in his car. Although I'd love nothing more than to roll around with him in the backseat of his BMW, it could get very complicated. Especially if he ignores me afterward or, even worse, wants to date me.

"No thanks," I say, standing up.

"But . . . how are you going to get home?"

"Don't worry about it."

"I'm not worried," he says. "I'm just curious."

"Thanks for lunch." I walk to the trash, dumping my tray before heading for the door.

"Anytime," Cameron calls after me. And it sounds like an offer.

When I get outside, the sun is shining. I'm glad because that means Cameron won't see me walking in the rain and I can spare myself the humiliation.

I'm just about to step off the curb into the parking lot when a white truck cuts across the lane and pulls up, nearly close enough to hit me. I jump back and gasp.

"*Slut*ton," Patrick calls, leaning out the driver's side window. My heart begins to race as I look from side to side, trying to decide if I should start walking or go back inside.

"Get in the truck," Patrick calls, shifting into park.

"Fuck off," I say, but my wrist tingles where he grabbed me

at the mall. I can still see the hate in his expression when he pulled me over the table.

"You owe me an apology." He's smiling, but his eyes are sinister. My gaze travels to his hand where it lies on the steering wheel. Even from here I can see the dark pink-and-purple scar. I wonder if it still hurts and if that's why he's such a raving asshole.

"Drop dead," I tell him, and start walking. I just need to stay away from him.

The engine of the truck revs so loudly it makes me jump. Panic breaks across my chest.

"I said, get in," Patrick calls.

Yeah, right. So I can end up in a ditch somewhere? I don't think so. I begin to walk faster, but no matter how quickly I go, his truck speeds up to stay at my side. My face is on fire, and my stomach is threatening to throw up the chicken nuggets I just ate.

What is he going to do to me? I stop and turn, walking back the way I came. Patrick brakes violently, thrown off by my movement. I listen as he tries to turn around. I know it'll be hard because the parking lot is narrow and Patrick drives something big to make up for a less-than-impressive package.

Relief washes over me when Cameron steps out of McDonald's, sipping from his drink and completely oblivious to my terror.

"Cameron," I call, jogging toward him. He turns to me, looking surprised at first, but then smiling.

"Change your mind about walking?"

The engine revs again, and my heart races. I'm afraid Patrick will grab me and throw me into his truck. That I'll become a story on the ten o'clock news.

The white truck is next to me again, but I don't look over. I keep my gaze trained on Cameron, and he glances over at the truck suspiciously. Patrick slows, but I walk faster.

"You *will* apologize," he yells out the open passenger window. "I'll be seeing you around, *Slut*ton."

He peels out with a loud squeal, and I stop walking, catching my breath. If it weren't for that grab at the mall, I would have told him all the different ways he could fuck himself, but now I don't. He's pissed, and he wants revenge. And to be honest . . . I don't know what to do about it. It makes me feel helpless.

"Who the hell was that?" Cameron asks when I reach him. He looks unnerved but in an "it's not really my business but I don't like it at all" sort of way.

"Him?" I say as if I hadn't noticed a guy harassing me. Cameron narrows his eyes and sips from his drink. I look away. "Don't know."

"Can I drive you home now?" Cameron asks.

"Are you sure you don't mind?" I hate myself for taking the ride, but I know Patrick might look for me. And I don't want to be available for street-side kidnapping.

"Of course I don't mind," Cameron says, walking to the trash can and tossing his soda in. "I wouldn't have fucking offered in the first place if I did."

I close my eyes for a second, wanting to stop the panic in my chest. I open them before Cameron notices. I let Patrick get inside my head. He's such a douchebag and I let him intimidate me.

Cameron begins walking to his car, and I watch after him, wondering if he'll look back at me, but he doesn't. He's not going to keep asking. I put my head down and follow behind him.

When I stop at the passenger door, our eyes meet as we both look over the roof of the car. His face is serious and beautiful. He smiles softly, as if he knows more about my situation than he'll say. Then he ducks down and gets into the driver's seat.

We drive quietly for a while. I'm used to driving with Travis and Retha, and with them it's rarely silent.

"Why don't you listen to the radio?" I ask Cameron.

He looks at me, then back at the road. "You want the radio on?"

"I just asked why you don't listen to it."

"I listen to it all the time."

"Not when I'm in here you don't."

He laughs. "Sutton, if you want to listen to the radio, turn it on."

"I don't want to," I say, shrugging. "I just thought it was strange."

"Strange?"

"Yeah."

"Okay. Yes, I'm a total weirdo who hates music in the car."

"Fine." I glance out the window, watching as the neighborhood becomes increasingly shabby. Shame sweeps over me again.

Cameron clears his throat, and I know that throat clearing is always the beginning of an awkward moment.

"Want to go somewhere?" he asks. I turn and find him staring out the windshield, looking more nervous than he sounds.

"I already went somewhere with you, remember?"

"I remember," he says casually. "But I thought you might be curious to see where I live."

"And why would you think that?" I realize that I sort of am. And I can't believe he'd even think of taking me there.

"Well, are you?" His lips have a small curve as he continues not to look at me.

Outside the window, the houses seem empty and desperate. Evan has a dentist appointment and won't be home until after six. My father will be at work—maybe. There's no one home but the ghost of my mother.

"I shouldn't," I say, continuing to watch the neighborhood. I try to think of all the reasons I have to say no, but I don't have any. "Will you take me home after?" I ask, turning to him.

"No. You'll have to walk." Cameron looks sideways at me and laughs. "Yes, Savannah. I will take you home whenever you want."

I nod and go back to watching the passing houses.

CHAPTER EIGHT

When we turn onto his street, I'm already completely uncomfortable. I've never been to this part of town, not even for a doctor's appointment. This is where celebrities would live if there were any around here. I feel unworthy.

Cameron pulls into a driveway that ends with three garage doors and is attached to a huge house with two-story windows. Cameron cuts the engine.

"Your house?" I ask.

"Yep."

"It's nice," I say as if I'm not at all impressed. I lean forward to look up at it through the windshield. "A bit on the small side."

"I don't hear that often," he says. When I look over he laughs like he's not just talking about his house. "Are we going inside?" he asks.

I sweep my eyes over the brick front, wondering why he brought me here, wondering why I agreed.

"Sure," I say, because he was right. I am curious to see where he lives.

Cameron gets out, but I stay in my seat a moment longer, watching him walk around the car and up to the front door. He doesn't turn around, and I like the ease with which he moves. He belongs here, in a place like this. I don't.

He leaves the front door open as he walks in, so I figure I might as well follow him. When I get out of the car, I glance around the neighborhood. An old lady walking by with two puffy white dogs waves at me. I freeze. Does she think I live here? Does she really not know her neighbors? I wave back.

"Sutton?" Cameron sings from inside the house. "You're letting all the heat out."

I decide to take him up on this adventure, and I walk down the pathway and inside the house.

Holy shit. It's nice. I close the door and look around at the dark wood floors, leather furniture, and gray painted walls. I feel underdressed in jeans and a T-shirt. I should probably take my shoes off. I hesitate because my socks don't match, but I don't want to be rude. I carefully place my sneakers behind the door.

Cameron walks out from what I assume is the kitchen, holding two cans of soda. He looks happy that I'm here, and now that I'm inside his warm house, I sort of feel that way, too. But I don't want him to know.

"I like your furniture," I say. Dumb.

"Uh . . . thanks." He hands me a Coke. Cameron looks down at my mismatched red and blue socks but doesn't mention them. "Do you want to see the rest of the house?" he asks.

"Showing off?"

"I have a heated pool." Cameron's grinning. He can tell that I don't give a shit that he has a pool, even a heated one. He's making fun of himself and I think it's sweet.

"Wow," I say, popping the top of my can. "Is it inground?"

"Uh, it's *indoor*."

First of all, I didn't even know that was possible. "Does it have a slide?" I ask.

"Nope," he replies. "My parents didn't want to look pretentious."

I laugh, and Cameron sips from his soda as we stand in his entryway. And just before it gets really uncomfortable, he motions to the hallway behind me. "You want to see my bedroom?" he asks.

I'm struck with a combination of desire and anger. Sure, I know I'm probably not the first girl he brought to lunch and then back to his bed. But it doesn't mean I want to be one of them. I don't need that sort of drama. I have enough of that with my current ex.

"Don't look at me like that," Cameron says, taking another sip of his Coke. "I'm not putting the moves on you. My room is more comfortable than out here." He nods to the immaculate living room. "I'm just being polite," he adds.

I don't doubt his sincerity, but I still don't understand it. "Why?" I ask him.

He furrows his brow. "Why not?"

"Because."

"You are very articulate in your arguments, you know that?"

"Fuck off."

"Sutton," he warns. "Remember to manage the anger."

It's a pretty good comeback, and my distrust eases. "Fine," I tell him, and exhale dramatically. "Show me your stupid room."

"Oh, now it's stupid?"

"Shut up. Just show me."

He bites his lip, spinning in his bright white athletic socks, and walks down the hall. I follow him, eyeing the artwork and family pictures on the wall. He's an only child. And it makes me remember what it was like when I was the only child in my family. My mom was around. My dad was sober. But I didn't have Evan, so I'd take now over then any day.

Cameron opens a door near the end of a short hall and steps aside for me to walk in first. He stares at the side of my face as I move past him. I stop as soon as I enter. His room is nicer than any bedroom I've seen before. I really shouldn't be here.

He closes the door, and I look back at him, alarmed. We're alone in his room with the door shut and no one home. This is clearly hookup territory. I'm not prepared for that. Not with him. Not with someone like him.

I begin to walk around, looking at all of his stuff. The papers on his dresser, a watch, postcards from California.

"You can sit down," Cameron says, motioning toward the bed. Nice try.

I raise my eyebrows at him, and he chuckles to himself.

"Do you give everyone this hard of a time or am I special?

Because I'm only suggesting you sit, instead of pacing my room like a caged lion. But if that's a dick thing to say, then I'm—"

I sit down on his bed, and he snaps his mouth shut. I'm not sure of the answer to his question. Most people I tell off deserve it. As for him being special . . . I don't think it matters.

Of course, his bed is the ultimate in comfort. Like one of those pillowy ones. I put my soda on his side table, and when I look at Cameron, he smiles. "What?" I ask. He's leaning against his dresser, his hair pushed back behind his ears.

He shrugs. "Nothing."

We're both quiet, and I don't even know where to start with talking to him. I feel so thrown in his place, so not in control. Seeing someone's bedroom for the first time is . . . intimate. Just thinking the word makes me blush.

"So can I sit next to you, or will you think I'm hitting on you, Miss Everybody Wants Me?" Cameron asks.

"It depends. Are you hitting on me?"

"No," he says. "I'm really not."

There's a sliver of disappointment, and I look down at my lap. "It's your house," I say.

"You're being so defensive," Cameron says. "I'm not the enemy. You don't have to fight with me." The bed shifts next to me, and although he's not touching me, I can feel the warmth from his body. I swallow hard.

"Maybe I only know how to fight."

"And maybe I'm fighting on the same side as you."

I like him. I do. And even though he's giving off the vibe

that he likes me back, it doesn't mean anything. Patrick used to tell me that he loved me in one breath and then tell me to "not look so poor" in the next. He'd whisper sweet words into my ear and put his hand down my pants, only to make me walk home because he was going out with his friends. I wasn't exactly the best judge of character back then. I can't be stupid like that again. Even though I know Cameron is cool, sweet even, I'm the one who will end up getting hurt. I'm the one with too much to lose.

"You're awfully quiet," Cameron says, sounding amused. Can he tell he makes me nervous?

"That's because you talk too much," I say.

"Only to you."

My face tingles. I can feel myself beginning to completely overanalyze the situation. Why does he talk to me? Why *me*?

"You're quiet again," Cameron says.

I have to say something to break this tension. He's within touching distance. "So . . ." I start. "You're super rich." It comes out like an accusation rather than a statement.

"No," he says. "But my parents are."

I turn and find him smiling down at his expensive-looking rug.

"Are they assholes?" I ask.

"Who?" He laughs. "My parents?" He sounds surprised by the question.

I guess they're not. "Never mind," I say quickly.

"No, it's okay," Cameron says, touching my hand. It's an innocent gesture, but I can't help pulling away and folding my hands on my lap.

"They're good people," Cameron adds. "Especially my mom."

I don't know why, but this makes me even more attracted to him. Something about the way his voice softens when he mentions his mom. I wish I could feel like that about my mom.

I want to know more about him. I want to understand him the way I do my friends. "Cameron," I say, looking sideways at him. "Why did you really trash the school?"

"It's a long, tragic story—"

"I'm serious. I want to know."

He turns suddenly to me, running his gaze over my face. I lick my lips as if anticipating him kissing me.

"I was mad," he says instead. "I was . . . pissed off and mad."

"Why?"

"Because I hated them. Langston Prep," he says. "I didn't belong there."

"You do drive a BMW." I know of Langston. It has a campus with trees and private sports teams. Having a nice car is a prerequisite.

"I wasn't like them," he says. "They were fake, and I'm not like that."

Cameron isn't calm and smiling. His eyes are narrowed and his lips are pulled up in a sneer. I shift a little closer to him, sort of fascinated by his anger.

"You could've done your thing and gone home," I say. "That's what I do now."

"See, that's the problem," he says. "School's not my thing, especially there. I hated it—sitting and listening to useless shit all day. I didn't want to go anymore.

"But my dad . . . he wouldn't let me drop out. He kept giving the school money to let me stay, even though I hardly showed up. The dean couldn't stand me. So then I had all these pricks telling me how grateful I should be that I was still allowed to attend. Like I owed them something when my dad was the one paying for their library."

Cameron rakes his fingers through his hair as I wonder what the going rate for a library is. He shakes his head.

"When I started hanging out with the 'scholarship kids,' as they liked to call them, the administration dragged me into a meeting. Talking about bad influences. Telling me that I was looking for trouble."

"Were you?" I like that he doesn't care. I like that he's not sorry.

He nods. "Maybe a little. But they had no right to tell me who to hang out with. They even rearranged my schedule. It was total bullshit. Then the dean, or as I called him to his face, Captain Douchebag, said if he saw me with Marcus and them again, he'd suspend me."

"Could he do that?"

"He did."

That's unfair. Why do they have the right to tell Cameron who he can be friends with? Then I realize that I'd be one of the people he was supposed to stay away from.

"So you got suspended?" I ask.

"Yep."

"Bastards," I say. His eyes are intense, and we're both breathing quickly.

"Bastards," he repeats softly as if he thinks it's cool that I said it.

If I lean toward him, will he kiss me? He's looking at me like he might. But maybe it would just turn into one of those really awkward, slow-motion moments of horror. A hug-kiss. A mis-understanding of signals. Oh, hell. I'm overanalyzing again.

"Then what happened?" I ask, trying to get him talking again. "What made you decide to trash the school?"

"I wanted out. I tried to tell my dad, have him yank his money from the place. But he wouldn't. He was convinced it was a good school. But screw that. I got my *bad influences* and we broke in."

"Weak-willed," I say.

"I guess."

"Hundred thousand?"

"Yep. Ransacked the administrative offices, broke shit, and destroyed their files." He looks in his lap. "Pissed in Captain Douchebag's coffeepot."

"Gross."

His eyes flick to mine. "You probably didn't need to know that part." I nod in agreement. "We were just angry," he adds.

"I think I can relate to angry."

He smiles. "I think you can, too."

"You did sort of overreact, though," I mention.

"This coming from the girl who used a pencil to stab someone."

"I had a good reason!"

"I did too."

"That's debatable."

"Yeah," he says. "It seemed like a great idea at the time. If I could go back, maybe I'd have handled it differently. Maybe I wouldn't have busted up the place. But I definitely would have still pissed in the coffeepot."

"Oh my God."

"Sorry."

I lean back on my hands, lounging. "Where are your bad influences now?" I ask. "How come they aren't at Brooks Academy?"

"They took off to California."

My mouth opens. "Are the police after them?"

"No," Cameron says. "I copped to it all, and my dad paid for the damages. He was embarrassed. Here he was, the school's biggest benefactor, and his fuckup son ruined the place. Made for some tense family dinners."

"I bet. Does he hate you now?"

"What? No, he's my father." His voice tells me he thinks it's a crazy statement. Obviously he's never met my father. And he never will.

"So tell me," I ask, "have you always been a trouble-maker?"

"Yep. Haven't you heard? Money doesn't buy happiness. Just really nice cars."

"Ah. I may have heard that somewhere."

Cameron sighs. "My father planned on me becoming a lawyer," he says. "But that's not me. I like doing what I want." He grins. "You know, like meeting girls at 7-Eleven and buying them Blow Pops."

"Lucky me."

"So lucky," he agrees.

"Why didn't you go to California with your friends?" I ask, even though I'm glad he didn't.

"My dad can be very persuasive." He pauses. "Wait, you trying to get rid of me, Sutton?"

"No," I say more seriously than I mean to.

"No?"

I need to straighten up, say something else to cover my admission of wanting him around, but I don't move. Then Cameron lies back on his bed, casually folding his hands behind his head, practically inviting me to climb on top of him. He's so damn smooth.

My fingers are trembling. We don't say anything, but we're staring at each other, maybe each of us wondering who'll make the first move. I think about lying next to him, shoulder to shoulder.

"Want to stay for dinner?" Cameron offers. He says it so casually, like we're regular people who spend entire days together all the time.

"I've got my own house," I say. "And, you might not know this about me, but I'm a master chef."

"Really?"

"You like mac 'n' cheese?" I ask.

He bites back his smile. "Sort of."

"Do you like hot dogs?"

He laughs. "No."

"Too bad. My dogs 'n' cheese are the best in town."

"Wow," he says, like he's impressed. "That . . . well, that sounds goddamn disgusting. You should definitely stay. We could get a pizza. Plus . . . it would really help me out. My mom wants to believe I'm well adjusted."

"Are you well adjusted?"

"No." He laughs. "I hate school. And you're my only friend there, so how about it? I'll owe you a favor."

Cameron's friends have left town without him. He must be lonely to want to talk to me. I don't want to go home yet . . . so I must be lonely too.

"Yeah, okay," I tell him. "I'll stay for dinner. Just don't make it weird."

He breaks into a huge smile and sits up, elbows on his knees. "You surprise me."

"You're making it weird."

His eyes flash with attraction—that look of an impending kiss. But I'm quick to dissolve it.

"So, pizza?" I ask.

"Actually"—he scrunches his nose apologetically—"I lied about that. My father hates pizza, so we never have it."

"He sounds like a monster."

A door closes, and both of us look toward the hall. "Cameron?" a woman calls from beyond the room. Her heels click along the wood floor.

I gasp and take Cameron's arm. He looks down to where I'm holding his biceps, and then he slowly raises his eyes until they meet mine. Our touch is fire, and I pull back my hand.

"I'm in here, Mom," he calls, although he's still looking at me.

"Is she going to freak?" I ask.

Cameron furrows his brow. "About what?"

"Me. Being in here alone with you."

"I'm allowed to have friends in my room," he says.

I feel stupid and lower my eyes. *Friends*. He didn't plan to hook up with me—he told me as much earlier. I misunderstood this moment.

The door opens.

"Oh," his mother says, looking between me and Cameron. "Sorry, I didn't know you had company."

I stare at her, waiting for her to kick me out. But she smiles warmly and it throws me off.

"I'm Kendra," she says, sticking out her hand and walking toward me. I stand awkwardly, feeling guilty. I can't imagine how much worse I'd feel if Cameron and I had been making out.

I shake her hand. "Savannah," I say, but I whisper it. What the hell is up with my voice? I haven't been doing anything wrong.

"It's nice to meet you." Kendra is pretty for someone's mother. Her shoulder-length blond hair is brushed smooth with the ends flipped up, and she smells like flowers.

"Savannah's in my class," Cameron says from behind me. When he asked me to stay for dinner, I hadn't considered this part. The part where his parents would find out I'm a delinquent too.

"Really?" Kendra puts her hands on her hips, like this is interesting trivia about me. "What did you do, honey?"

Cameron laughs. "She stabbed her ex-boyfriend."

Kendra shakes her head. "Oh, stop," she tells him, slapping his shoulder. "That's not funny."

I'm glad she doesn't believe him, but I'm going to kill him later anyway. Kendra turns to me.

"Are you staying for dinner?" she asks.

"Oh, uh . . ." I plan to back out, but Cameron goes to stand next to his mother and smiles, like he knows I'm having second thoughts. Does he really want me to stay? To have dinner with his family? What kind of psychopath is he?

I still have plenty of time to get home before Evan. I could walk out the door.

"Please?" Cameron says simply. And I can see that he truly wants me to, free of manipulation. It's raw. It's honest. So I decide to do him this favor. After all, he'll owe me. And who knows, Retha and I might need a getaway car again soon.

"My brother gets home at six," I say. "I have to be home before then."

"Perfect," Kendra says, clapping her hands together. "We like to eat early. We're ordering Cantonese."

"Savannah loves Cantonese," Cameron says, smiling at me. He's thrilled that I'm staying. It's boyish and cute, maybe a little cocky.

"Great," I say to Kendra, although I've never heard of Cantonese food.

"Would you mind helping me, Savannah?" Kendra asks, motioning toward the kitchen.

"Uh . . . okay," I say. I'm not sure what she needs help with. I thought she was ordering in.

"Cameron," she says, looking over her shoulder at him. "Call Daddy and see when he'll be home."

"Fun," he answers.

As Cameron takes out his phone to call, Kendra leans her shoulder into mine. "It's nice to see Cameron has friends again," she whispers to me. "I've been worried about him."

She leaves to head toward the kitchen, and I steal one more glance at Cameron. He's talking to his dad, sounding annoyed, but he must sense me because he looks over. He starts to smile, and I feel it in my heart. Right where it hurts.

So I turn away and follow his mother into the kitchen.

CHAPTER NINE

The Cantonese food arrives in fancy plastic serving trays instead of paper bags. And yet Cameron's mother still has me help her put it in porcelain dishes before setting it on the table.

The dining room is really nice with a cabinet full of shiny glasses, tall-backed chairs, and a shimmery light fixture hanging above us. The table was already set when I walked in; they keep plates on it even when no one is home.

Cameron sits across from me at the table, which means I'll have to look at him all through dinner. Cameron's father got home around four, and now he and Kendra are at opposite heads of the table. It's awkward, the way we sit like a family, as if we're on a TV show.

Marcel, Cameron's father, doesn't look like a typical rich asshole. He's big, like a football player, and his hair is dark, brushed back, and long. He's handsome, but in a much harder way than Cameron. And he's wearing a dark blue suit. Even at the dinner table, he's wearing a suit. I guess that's sort of assholish.

"So, Savannah," Marcel asks in between bites. "Do you have any brothers or sisters?"

It's a question I dread because I feel like people should know about Evan's disability, but I hate defining him by it. He's perfect the way he is. I don't want people to feel sorry for him. He doesn't need their pity.

"I have a brother," I say, pushing the food around on my plate. Cameron's in my class, so he's already heard about Evan. But it doesn't make it any easier to talk about him now.

"A brother," Kendra says. "Is he younger?"

"Yeah. He's seven."

She makes a noise that can only be described as glee, and I want to leave. Tension squeezes my shoulders, and I wonder how I can escape this conversation.

"That's sweet," Kendra says. "I teach third grade at McKinley. What school does he go to?"

There's a stinging in my eyes. People don't ask me these sorts of questions anymore. I've forgotten how to answer them. "He goes to Tomlinson," I say. The only "special" school in the area.

"That's a nice school," Cameron's mother says gently.

Marcel picks up his wineglass and takes a sip, avoiding my eyes. Kendra looks like she wants to know more but knows it's rude to ask.

"What's his name?" Cameron asks, startling me.

"Evan."

"That's adorable," Kendra says.

I watch Cameron, comforted by him—comforted that he asked for my brother's name. It feels like he's the only person in the world who understands, but really, I know he doesn't. How could he?

I drop my eyes to my plate, suddenly missing Evan, and feeling guilty for eating this nice food without him. "He's with our aunt Kathy," I say, although no one asked. "She takes him a few days a week."

The room is quiet and heavy. I'm no longer hungry. I want Kathy to bring Evan home so that I can hug him. He's a tough responsibility, but he's mine. I'm empty without him.

Suddenly, Cameron laughs like he just thought of something. I look up at him, and when I do, he grins and turns to his mother.

"Savannah was wondering about our pool," he says. "And we decided that I should have a pool party."

My mouth drops open, but Kendra chuckles as if she knows Cameron is (mostly) joking.

"Really?" Marcel asks. "Then I should thank you, Savannah. Cameron hasn't used the pool in months. It's a great idea."

My eyes are wide. "But I didn't—"

"I'll have one on Saturday," Cameron interrupts. "Soon enough?" He's trying to be cute, which he is, but right now it's not enough. Talking about Evan has reminded me of my life. My limitations.

I don't respond, looking down at my noodles instead. There's no way I can come to Cameron's party. I don't know what sort of people will be there, or what they'll think of me. Especially if some of them are from Langston Prep. I'll just be another "scholarship kid" to them.

"I'll order the food," Kendra says happily. She and Marcel begin to make plans, talking about a caterer.

Cameron's foot bumps mine under the table and subtly rests there. I look up at him just as he puts a forkful of rice in his mouth. Neither of us acknowledges that we're touching. My heart beats a little faster, and I go back to eating my food.

After dinner I see that it's nearly six and ask Cameron to drive me home. I say good-bye to his parents, thanking them again for dinner. Kendra seems sad to see me go. Cameron grabs my shoes for me, and I still can't believe how comfortable he is with me around his family. Other than Retha's, I've never really gotten along with parents.

It's not raining, so Cameron gets the full view of my neighborhood. I twist my hands around the strap of my backpack resting at my feet. I'm embarrassed, especially after seeing where he lives. Right now my ramshackle white house looks more like an abandoned building. I hate going home.

My father's car is in the driveway, and I glance at the clock, worried that Evan got home before me. But it's not quite six.

"Thanks for the all-day feasting," I say, looking over at Cameron.

"No problem," he says. "Thanks for letting me pretend I have friends."

"Yeah, about that. Do you really not have friends?"

He furrows his brow. "Do you think I don't have any friends?"

"I don't know. I mean . . . just answer the question. Do you?"

"Of course I do. I'm not a fucking loser. I just don't have any friends at Brooks. At least until now."

"I'm sure you wouldn't have had a problem finding more." I don't like that idea, but I know it's true—with his looks, his money, Cameron could be with anybody.

"I doubt they'd be as interesting as you," he says.

"You're sort of interesting too," I murmur. "For a trouble-maker."

He smiles and rests his head back on his seat. "You sure you have to go in?" he asks. "We can just sit here for a while. Talk."

My body tingles for his quiet voice in my ear. If things were different, if *I* were different, I'd stay with him. Even leave with him. But I can't. "Thanks, again," I say, and pull on the door handle.

His hand grazes mine on the seat as I get out, maybe reaching for me, maybe accidentally. But I slam the door and jog up the driveway, trying to catch my breath.

On my way to the house, I hear his window roll down.

"Hey," Cameron calls. "If you're interested, I know about a kickass pool party this weekend."

I turn, walking backward so I can face him. "I'll think about it," I say.

"Have a good night, Sutton."

"You too."

When I get inside my house, I lean back against the door

and close my eyes. Sure, Cameron called me interesting, but he doesn't know me or my life. He's never seen Evan melt down or my father scream. And I won't let him. I'll never let him see that part of me. I bring my hand to my chest, remembering what it felt like when he touched me. And wishing I stayed in his car just a little longer.

"Where were you?" The sound of my father's voice startles me, and I look over to find him in the living room, the curtains drawn and glow of the TV painting his silhouette. I know Evan's not home because he would have run to me the minute the door opened.

"I was out," I say, and quickly straighten my back, ready to ignore him.

"Savannah," he says, but this time there's a question in his voice, like he wants to talk to me. Panic immediately begins to crawl up my throat.

"What?" I ask, stopping at the entrance of the room. "It's none of your business where I was."

"I'm your father."

"Sure, whatever that means."

The image on the TV switches, bathing him in a blue light. He doesn't look well. I have a pang of sympathy before I remind myself of what a shitty human being he is.

"I spoke to a lawyer today," he says quietly. My heart dips, and I clutch onto the wall where I'm leaning. "Kathy paid for a family attorney. They have a good case for custody."

It shocks me, the fact that my aunt would go that far. "But you told them no, right?" I ask.

"I told them I needed to think about it."

"What's there to think about?" I walk into the room and stop in front of him. "You don't just give away your children."

"You know it's not that simple."

"It can be," I say. I stare him down, wishing I was the one with a lawyer, wishing I could be the one fighting to keep Evan to myself. I'm the person who loves him most. I'd do anything for him. Our father can't say the same thing.

"You tell them no, Dad," I say, turning my back on him and starting toward my room. "You fight for your son or I swear to God"—I pause at my bedroom door—"I'll never forgive you."

And with that I walk into my room, my fear suffocating me. A lawyer. Kathy has crossed the line this time. I was stupid to let her have an extra day with Evan. Now I know better.

I pause against my door, looking around my room. My mind turns back to Cameron—how normal I felt today with him, even if it was totally weird. And in a way, I want to go to his stupid party this weekend. I've never been in an indoor pool before.

Desperate for a distraction, I rush over to my dresser and search for my bathing suit. When I find it, I hold it up, trying to decide if it will even fit anymore. But as I examine the faded red fabric, the fantasy comes to a screeching halt. I toss my bathing suit on top of my dresser and swing around to look at my bedroom with its old furniture and worn sheets. I sit on my bed and look down at my mismatched socks, scared to imagine that things can get better.

* * *

Evan's in a good mood when Kathy arrives to drop him off. I
wait for him on the porch, giving him a big hug the moment
I see him. He tells me he doesn't have any cavities, which I
take complete credit for. I'm the one who makes him brush
his teeth every night.

Kathy gets out of her minivan, and my chest wells up with
anger at the sight of her. I force a smile and look down at
Evan. He holds up a small plastic bag with a new toothbrush
and a tube of toothpaste.

"You should go show Daddy what you got from the dentist," I say. "He'll be impressed to hear how great it went. I'll
meet you there in a second." Evan nods and rushes inside the
house, excited to have brought home a gift bag from the den-
tal hygienist. His happiness is almost enough to thaw me out,
but when I see Kathy climbing the porch steps, I freeze solid.

"A lawyer?" I snap. "You got a fucking lawyer, Kathy?"

Her lips pucker in disapproval of my language, but she's
better at keeping her temper than I am. "She's Evan's lawyer," Kathy says. "She wants what's best for him."

I scoff. "Oh, yeah. Sure. And you happen to be the one
paying her bill so I wonder who she thinks is best. This is
low," I tell her, taking a step forward. I expect her to back up,
but she doesn't. She holds my gaze steady.

"I just want him to have a good home," she says.

"He has me. I'm his home."

She blinks, seeming moved by my statement. Maybe even
ashamed. But I won't let her trick me into giving up custody
of my brother. Getting a lawyer, knowing I couldn't afford

to do the same . . . I have no trust in her anymore. She's a judgmental bitch. And she's not getting Evan.

"You can't see him anymore," I say, crossing my arms over my chest.

Kathy's eyes flash with anger, but she quickly pulls it back. "Legally," she says, "you can't make that call, Savannah." She lets the words soak in, demolishing my argument.

"Now," she says, sounding confident. "I'll be here on Thursday. Tell Evan I said good night." She knows she's right—my opinion wouldn't hold up in court. I would need my father to side with me, and he isn't exactly listening anymore.

When I get back inside, I find Evan and our dad in the living room. Evan is going on about the dentist, how scary it was but how the dentist told him he had smiling eyes. My father laughs a little, and I feel myself flinch, like somehow, I expect him to always be awful. At this point, it's harder when he's not.

I wait, my shoulder against the doorway, for them to finish talking. I haven't seen Evan in four days, and I'm anxious to have him with me again. But I give them this moment.

When Evan is done with the story, I wave him over to me and hug him. Our father goes out to the driveway to work on his truck.

"I hated this weekend without you," I tell Evan, gathering him up in my arms. "You know how boring and dumb Dad can be." Evan laughs, that sort of infectious laugh that brightens any room. "Did you have fun at Aunt Kathy's?" I ask, bringing him to sit on the couch. I wonder if he talked to the lawyer too, if my aunt involved him at all. But he doesn't mention it, and my brother can't lie.

"Murdock licked my face," Evan says, widening his eyes as he gets ready to delve into every pointless detail. My aunt's dog, Murdock, is a big, white beast of an animal. I used to love playing with him. But now I'm jealous because although I want Evan to have fun—want it more than anything—I wish it could be with me. I wish I didn't have to work so hard just to have simple moments like this. "He's a good boy." Evan sounds just like our uncle Donavon. "But Murdock can't have broccoli." I imagine my brother fed him his share of vegetables whenever he could.

I sit on the couch and listen as Evan tells me the rest of his weekend adventures, which include a trip to the mall for new sneakers and a movie. I've never heard of the cartoon he saw, and for that matter, I can't even remember the last time I went to a movie; I was probably with Patrick.

When my brother is done, I ask him to take out his homework. The assignments are modified so he can supposedly complete them on his own, but he never can. I help him with the worksheet, and at bedtime, when Evan comes to snuggle up in my bed, I brush his too-long hair and read him a story—same story every time. He listens, quiet and sweet. Just before he drifts off, leaving me to carry him back to his room, he whispers that he loves me. And I tell him that I love him too.

CHAPTER TEN

"I can't believe you went to Cameron Ramsey's house," Retha says, looking back at me from the front seat. The sun is shining bright this morning, and it's almost enough to make me feel hopeful. "But really," she says, "the bigger crime here is that you didn't jump his sexy-ass bones."

"Do you actually mean the things you say?" I ask her, smiling sweetly.

"Absolutely. He's hot, Savvy."

"Hey," Travis says, taking his eyes off the road to look at her.

"Aw . . . I'm sorry, baby." She leans over and pecks his lips. "I mean he's hot for Savvy's standards."

"Right," Travis says. We all know that Cameron's hot by anyone's standards. But when Travis glances back at me to grin, I notice the dark circles and pale skin. I'd hoped a day away would have cleared things up a little. Instead, he looks worse.

"So, um . . ." I start. "How did it go yesterday?"

Retha looks at Travis, and then turns toward the window. I feel the air thicken in the car. "Bad," she says quietly.

I'm not sure if she means the hearing or if Travis got high. Possibly both. Retha and I tell each other nearly everything, but when it comes to Travis's addiction . . . neither of us is entirely upfront. But I'm sick of being left out of this conversation.

"Are you using again?" I ask Travis, meeting his eyes in the mirror. I feel Retha turn to me, probably surprised that I'd just come out and ask.

Travis swallows hard and shakes his head. "Don't turn this into an NA meeting, Savannah," he says. "I'm just in a shitty mood. My dad's coming home this week." He pauses and stares out the windshield. "Ain't the justice system grand?"

"Travis, I—"

"I'm good," he says. "I promise."

He glances back at me and smiles. But my face stings. He promised last time too. Exact words. There's a chill down my back as Travis focuses on driving. I look at his arms, but they're covered with long sleeves. I swallow down my fear and wait for my heart to slow. I wait for denial to kick in.

By the time we pull into the school lot, the three of us are joking again—even if it's hollow. Retha schemes how to hook me up with Cameron. Now that she knows why he's at Brooks, minus the personal details, she likes him that much more. He's one of us.

Retha can barely contain her excitement as we walk into class. "And you know I'm going to that party with you," she says, weaving her head like I'm about to fight her on the issue. But I'm glad she'll be there with me. I mean . . . if I go at all.

Travis doesn't say much and heads straight to his desk. I watch after him, and then I notice that Cameron isn't here. I wonder where he is.

"I've got just the right bikini for this," Retha continues. "Those prep boys won't even know what to do with themselves."

I smile. "I think we both know what they'll be doing with themselves." We both crack up. "Besides," I say, "I'm not sure I should go. I don't belong there."

"Oh, no," she says. "You're going to that party. You deserve to be happy, Savvy. Stop trying to mess it up."

"You just want to show off in your bathing suit."

"Hell yes, I do. So don't ruin this for me." But I know she's mostly kidding. She wants what's best for me. It helps when it's fun for her, too.

We're all a little surprised when Mr. Jimenez walks in with his leather bag and sets it on his desk. We were kind of hoping to have a substitute or even another shortened class.

"Hey, Mr. Jimenez," Gris calls out. "How'd jury duty go? Did you get the gig?"

"Sorry, no," he answers, taking off his glasses to clean them.

We groan our disappointment. Jury duty is almost like being famous. At least around here.

"Why not, man?" Gris asks. "You'd be perfect for it. Hell, you work here."

Mr. Jimenez puts his glasses back on, his expression serious. "Exactly the problem," he says. "I knew the defendant."

We all go quiet, and I silently take stock of the classmates who left at the beginning of the year. Their faces blur together and it's a reality check. It doesn't matter who it was because it could be any of us.

Retha goes to her seat, and a second later Cameron walks in the door, and my heartbeat skips. He murmurs hello to me, simple, like I didn't just have dinner with his family last night. I'm not sure what I expect him to say.

Mr. Jimenez looks at Cameron, and then at the rest of us. He slaps his hands together. "There is some good news, though," our teacher says. "Field trip time."

Several people cheer, but Mr. Jimenez is quick to squash our dreams. "Don't get too excited," he says. "We're just going to the computer lab."

I groan. The computer lab sucks. The Internet connection is on the school server, which blocks anything good. The only time we use it is when there's a major assignment or dreaded test prep.

We end up having to split into two groups, and of course, I'm in the one with Gris and not Retha, Travis, or Cameron. The day is long, and I begin clicking random bubbles to get through the test faster. I'll take my time on the *actual* GED.

We're all tired at the end of the day, and when I return to class, Cameron is already gone. I'm a little disappointed. What if he changed his mind about the party? What if he changed his mind about me?

Retha and Travis waited for me, and the three of us head out. Travis says that he'll drive us to the party on Saturday; he doesn't ask for an invite, even though I'm sure Cameron would have no problem with him being there. It's Travis—he doesn't want to be around people. I wonder how much worse he will get once his father is home.

"I'll bring the groceries by later," Retha says to me as I climb out of the car.

"Sounds good. Thank you." They leave, and I go to the curb to wait for Evan's bus.

Evan doesn't have any homework, so I let him color while I go to the kitchen to make dinner. Although the food I bought was for him, I couldn't get nearly as much as I'd hoped. Retha will drop off the bag of groceries her mom grabbed for me, one filled with cereal and canned goods. But for now I open a can of chicken noodle soup—extra noodles—and heat it up in a pan.

I take out Evan's favorite blue bowl from the cabinet and the chipped one for myself, and fill them. I grab both before heading into the living room. I set them on the coffee table and gather up Evan's crayons to put them back in their box. He scrunches his nose and crosses his arms over his chest. He looks just like me when he does.

He's upset, but I don't want to indulge him and make it worse. I ignore the start of his tantrum and sit on the floor in front of the couch. The soup is still hot, so I tell Evan to be careful, and blow on my spoonful before taking a sip.

"I don't want to eat this," Evan whines from behind me. "I want dogs 'n' cheese."

"I didn't have enough for hot dogs," I tell him. "This is what we have for now."

"Savannah." Evan's voice rises. "I want dogs 'n' cheese."

"Stop it," I say, sliding his bowl in front of him. "I told you I don't have any damn hot dogs. What do you want me to do?"

"Dogs 'n' cheese!" Evan shouts, kicking the coffee table with his new sneakers.

"Stop!" I yell, turning to look back at him. I put my hand on his knee, but he kicks again and knocks over his bowl of soup. The hot liquid pours onto my jeans, and I jump up.

"Damn it!" I yell, and swipe at my clothes. Evan starts to thrash on the couch, and I reach to take him by the shoulders. "Evan, knock it off."

He rips away from me, and his arm swings out and hits me in the mouth, pinching my lip against my tooth.

"Fuck," I say to myself. I touch my lip, and when I bring my fingers down, I see that I'm bleeding. All at once the exhaustion, old bruises, and loneliness collide. My eyes blur with tears, and I stand there as Evan slides off the couch onto the floor, sobbing and miserable. He calls for our mother.

I back away, tears trickling down my face. Evan will probably cry himself to sleep tonight. I'll probably do the same.

I wipe my cheeks and go into the kitchen to grab a piece of ice for my mouth. As I stand there at the freezer, I touch the cold cube to my lip with a wince.

There's a knock at the front door. I quickly cross the house to open it, passing by Evan, who's still crying on the floor. I'm relieved to find Retha on my porch, holding a brown grocery bag. Travis stands behind her.

"Jesus," Retha says when she sees the ice at my lip. "You all right?"

"Yeah," I say, and hold the door open to let them in. She pauses in front of me, gauging the situation.

"Your asshole father home?" she asks.

"No."

"Good." Retha heads inside and sets the groceries on the kitchen table. "And I brought those hot dogs."

She walks straight to the couch and sits near where Evan lies on the carpet. Travis takes the chair across from her, putting his sneaker on the edge of the coffee table and avoiding the spilled soup.

Retha tightens her jaw; I know she hates seeing Evan like this, but she's better at hiding it. She's better at playing tough. "What's going on, Evan?" she asks him. "Did you hit your sister again?"

Evan sniffles and lifts his eyes to look at Retha. She tilts her head, letting him know she's not messing around.

"Yes," he says quietly. He sounds sorry, and I lower the ice from my lip so he won't feel guilty.

"Why?" Retha asks him.

"I wanted hot dogs," he says, starting to cry again.

"No," she says, holding up a warning finger. "No crying. You need to apologize to Savannah. Right now."

Evan's unable to actually stop crying, but he looks over at me. "I'm sorry, Savvy," he says in his little voice.

"It's okay, buddy." His apology hurts my heart. "Just don't do it again."

He nods, and Retha reaches out her hand to him. "Come here," she says. Evan immediately climbs onto the couch and snuggles up to Retha. She kisses the top of his head.

"Hey, Evan," Travis says, leaning forward. "I brought you something."

Evan wipes his sleeve under his nose. "What?" he asks.

Travis pulls out a package of Hostess cupcakes from his jacket pocket, and my brother practically jumps out of Retha's arms. She's quick to grab the back of his shirt to stop him.

"Not so fast," she says. "First you need to clean up the mess you made."

His bottom lip juts out, and I worry that he'll have another tantrum, but he listens to Retha better than he listens to me. Evan gets on the carpet, and I help put the noodles in the tipped-over dish, while Travis grabs a towel from the kitchen to soak up the broth.

When it's cleaned, Evan waits patiently on the couch, his feet swinging because they don't reach the floor. Retha pretends to look him over like she's still deciding if he deserves it. Then she asks Travis for the cupcakes.

"You get *one*," she tells Evan.

"Right," I add. "The other will be in your lunch for tomorrow, okay?"

"Okay," he answers immediately, too excited to actually consider the consequences of having to wait.

Retha gives him a cupcake, and then me, her, and Travis head into the kitchen to put away the groceries. I set a pot of water on the stove and get out the hot dogs and mac 'n' cheese for dinner.

"You spoil him," Retha calls, sitting in my father's chair at the table. Travis puts the boxes of cereal in the cabinet.

"Hardly," I say. I lick my lower lip, tasting blood. Travis comes over to the stove and asks to look at it. He examines my lip and tells me that I shouldn't need stitches. We joke that he's the expert on stitches since he's had to get them too many times to count.

I must look pathetic though, because he wraps his arms around me and gives me a hug. His jacket smells like leather, smoke, and motor oil. It's a cologne all his own. I straighten and thank him. Times like this, you can't give in to the emotions of it all. It'll bury you.

My friends wait while I make dinner, and then I give them their own portion of food. All of us sit at the table, like a family—a dysfunctional one, but a family nonetheless. Evan smiles, looking around at us.

And I think that this can work out. When there's this much love, it has to work out.

CHAPTER ELEVEN

The week passes quickly. Cameron jokes with me a little in class, updating me on his preparations for the pool party. On Thursday I let Kathy take Evan, refusing to speak even a word to her when she does.

It's also the day Travis's dad comes home. But no one wants to talk about that. Doesn't mean I don't worry, though. Part of me hopes this will be the last time Travis's dad gets out—that next time he'll stay in jail. But it seems like the law only gets involved in our lives to ruin them.

By Saturday the scratches from the cornfield have healed, and I have only one new bruise—which will look awesome with my bathing suit.

My phone rings early in the morning and I dash out to answer it, worried it's Kathy and that something has happened to Evan. I pick up the phone and run my other hand through my tangled hair.

"Hello?" I ask, my voice thick with sleep.

"Savvy?" Retha chokes out. She's crying, and I tighten my grip on the phone, panic breaking across my chest.

"What's wrong?" I ask. "What's happening?" This is bad—Retha doesn't cry. Tear up, sure, but not sob cry. She'd rather punch something first.

"It's Travis," she says. "He's relapsed."

I let her words sink in, and my lips begin to tremble. I stagger back and bump against the living room wall. I *knew* it. I knew Travis was using again, but I didn't stop him. I didn't force him to talk about it. My face breaks, and I put my palm over my eyes. When we didn't go out last night, I figured he and Retha were together. "What happened," I murmur.

"After he dropped me off," Retha says, "he got into a fight with his dad. Bastard nearly broke his arm again—I can't believe he ever got paroled."

"Fuck," I whisper, hitching in a cry. "Who gave him the drugs?"

"He left his house and tracked down those assholes he used to hang out with—the ones from State Street. They got him a fix. He sat in their apartment and shot that shit into his arms." She starts to break down but bites it back. "His brother thought he was dead when he found him on the lawn this morning. Those junkies dumped him instead of taking him to the hospital." She pauses to breathe. "He OD'd this time, Savvy. His heart stopped."

Physical pain shakes me, and my entire body goes rigid, ready to convulse with tears. "Tell me he's okay," I whisper. "Please tell me he's okay, Retha." *Not Travis. Please, God, don't take Travis from us.*

Retha sniffles, as if my meltdown helped clear her head. "He's alive, Savvy. We won't know the extent of the damage for a while, but they got him to the hospital and were able to stabilize him. He's got a hell of an infection in his arm."

"Which hospital?" I dart my eyes around the house, thinking of how I can get to the hospital. I spy my father's keys hanging near the door, and I start that way.

"He's not there anymore," Retha says. "They've sent him to a rehab center in Cleveland. He's on lockdown in the infirmary—no visitors."

I clutch my father's keys in my hand, feeling the metal bite into my palm. "For how long?" I ask.

"He has to stay there a mandatory ninety days. And if he fucks up this time, he's going to prison for parole violation. This is his last chance." She pauses a long moment, her toughness fading with each jagged breath she pulls in. "He looked so bad at the hospital," she whispers. "It was like it wasn't him at all. I've never . . ." She breaks into a new cry. "I can't live without him, Savvy."

Soon her sobs are replaced with thuds, the sounds of her fist hitting things. The wall, maybe. The table.

"Stop," I tell her, although I know she won't listen. "I'm coming over. We can—"

"I'm leaving, Savvy," Retha says. "I'm on my way out right now."

My stomach drops, and I wipe hard at my cheeks. "What? Where are you going?"

"I'm going to my grandmother's out in Cleveland to wait for him. The lawyer told me he should be able to have visitors in a few weeks. And I have to be there for him—Travis needs me."

I drop my father's keys and walk over to the wall and lean against it, slowly sliding down until I'm resting on the faded carpet. There are no words that can make this better. The drugs have beaten Travis again. He won't graduate this year. Neither will Retha. And when Travis comes back, we'll wait to see if he'll relapse again. All we can do is wait. The drugs ruin all of us.

"I can't come with you," I say miserably. "I can't leave Evan."

"I know," she says. "And Travis will understand. I'll help him. I'll get him better and bring him home. I promise."

The word makes me cry. Travis promised too. Fear, dread, and loneliness all assault me at once, and I cover my face with my hand.

"When are you leaving?" I ask, sounding as controlled as I can manage.

"My uncle's on his way to pick me up," she says.

"What am I going to do without you guys?" I ask. Travis and Retha are all I have, other than Evan. I don't know how to lose them.

"You'll be okay," Retha says. "You're one tough bitch, Savvy." She laughs. "You put a fucking pencil through a football player's hand and punched out a girl in the cornfield. I don't need to worry about you."

I chuckle through my tears, knowing that I'm not nearly as tough as anyone thinks. Knowing that without Retha and Travis, I feel alone and vulnerable. "I'll miss you," I say. "I already miss you."

"Stop," she says, trying to sound light. "Three months. I'll be back in three months."

But three months is a long time. And I can't even let myself consider that it might be longer. "Evan will be sad," I say, looking toward my brother's closed bedroom door. How am I going to explain this to him? He adores Retha.

"Tell him I said that when I get back, I'm going to beat his little ass if he doesn't behave himself."

"Retha," I say.

"What?"

"Hurry up, okay?"

"I will."

"And tell Travis I love him and to hurry up, too."

"Definitely."

We wait a moment longer, and then Retha says good-bye and hangs up. I stay on the floor, still shaking.

I knew. I hate myself because I knew something was wrong with Travis, and I didn't stop this. Because he promised. He fucking promised me. And I was too worried about privacy to press for an honest answer. I might as well have put that needle in myself.

I begin to cry again, letting the knowledge slip over me. I. Am. Alone.

There's a noise behind my father's door, and I have to pull myself together before he gets up. I swipe under my eyes and slowly stand, hand on the wall.

Travis's life is hard. He has a dad who beats him and his mother is dead. It isn't fair, the way some of us have gotten so screwed by life. It isn't fair that someone as beautiful as Travis is haunted by addiction. That people always expect the worst of Retha, even though she's the best friend I could ever have.

At least I have Evan. No matter how shitty I think my life is, I have my brother. I'll always have him. And although he's the hardest part of my life, he's also the best. Because when Evan's happy, I'm happy. If only I can figure out how to keep him that way forever. How can I possibly make him happy in the awful place where we live?

I stumble to my room and close my door. I lean against it, completely overwhelmed, and notice my bathing suit lying across my dresser.

Cameron's pool party.

Retha wanted to go so badly; she even convinced me to go. It would have been the highlight of her week, checking out the hot rich boys, showing off in her bikini and making them drool.

But now, looking around at my shabby life, I know I've been delusional. This is what I have. All I have. And going to a stupid party isn't going to change that.

I choke back a cry and stomp over to swipe everything off my dresser, sending my bathing suit and a frame Evan made me to the floor. And then I collapse on my bed and cry.

CHAPTER TWELVE

I don't go to Cameron's party.

At school on Monday I'm miserable without Retha and Travis. I managed to collect enough change around my house to take the bus to school, but I'll have to find more if I hope to make it through the week. I sit in class, occasionally looking back at Travis's desk, my heart breaking every time I find it empty. Retha made it to Cleveland and gave me her grandmother's number. I wish I could talk to her now.

Cameron walks into class, and I'm not sure what I expected. I didn't think he'd ignore me. He does. His hair hangs close to his face and his black T-shirt is dark and crisp against his jeans when he takes off his coat.

I wait as he sits down, but he still doesn't say anything. He takes out his phone and begins texting, like I'm not three feet away, staring at him. My face stings a little, and I look down at my desk. Mr. Jimenez is late.

Five minutes pass. The anxiety in my chest is making me crazy. Cameron hasn't spoken to me. I stare at him again, practically begging him to notice me. I'm too emotionally raw for this shit. Finally I give in.

"I'm sorry I didn't go to your party," I say.

His thumbs stop on the phone, but he doesn't look up. "You weren't there?" he asks. "I didn't notice."

Ouch. "Was it fun?"

"Blast."

I don't know what else to say. He doesn't seem *mad* mad, which is weird because I sort of want him to be. I want him to ask for an explanation. I want an excuse to tell him about Retha and Travis—even though I won't tell him about Retha and Travis.

Cameron should be mad at me for making him have a party and then not showing up. But he just starts texting again.

Mr. Jimenez is now ten minutes late, which isn't cool. Because of the school's budget, we know subs are pretty much impossible. But . . . we count on him. Sure, we give our teacher a hard time, but we expect him to take it. We expect him to come back.

Gris and Lucinda stand up, exchanging a few words before leaving together. They're obviously hooking up; I'm not the slightest bit surprised. Although to be honest, she could do better. I look back toward Retha's desk to tell her, and when she's not there, it's a cold splash of reality.

I miss her—I miss Retha and Travis so much that it's hard to think about them. I just want my friends back. But Travis needs help and he'll get it. That's what matters. That's worth waiting for.

Their absence creates a fire, bravery in my chest. I have to be strong for them. I have to show them I'm all right. I look over at Cameron.

"Who do you text?" I ask him. It's a bold question and I regret it the second I ask. He looks sideways at me but doesn't answer.

He might be texting a girl—maybe one from his party. I bet she's a blonde, a cute, perky blonde. Jealousy squeezes my heart.

"I don't think we're having class," Cameron says. He slides his phone into the pocket of his jeans. "I'm going to take off."

"Good for you," I murmur. If my life hadn't completely blown up, I might have gone to the party. And sure, I wish I had. But now he's moved on. Didn't take him long. Obviously I hadn't been *that* interesting.

He stands, gathering his things before walking away. I feel rejected, but then halfway to the door, Cameron pauses to look back at me.

"You coming or not?" he asks.

I lift my eyes to his, startled. "What? Where?"

"I don't know. But I'm sure it'll be awesome. We can tell each other secrets and shit."

He wants me to leave with him. He must not hate me after all. And I'm lonely, scared. I need a distraction to pass the time until Retha and Travis get back. Cameron can be that distraction.

"Okay," I say. Cameron waits for me, and then together we walk out.

We don't say much on the way to his car, and despite the fact that he invited me along, the tension is thick. So the minute we get inside, I turn to him.

"Is this you getting back at me?" I ask.

"For what?"

It occurs to me that I'm overthinking again. He really might not have even noticed that I wasn't at his party. "Never mind," I say.

"No, really, Sutton. What would I be getting back at you for?" Cameron asks. "The fact that my parents rented tables and chairs? Or that my mom had it catered because she thought you loved Cantonese food?" His face grows serious. "Or maybe the fact that I waited by the door, checking every few minutes, to see if you were just too chickenshit to come inside?"

"Yeah. Any of those." Although I feel terrible, at the same time I'm glad he cares. I like how it makes me feel. "Did you really wait by the door for me?" I ask quietly.

"No."

"You did, didn't you?" I ask.

"For like a second." Cameron waves his hand as if I'm making a big deal out of nothing. "And to answer your question, no. I'm not getting back at you. I just . . . can we hang out?"

"I don't really like Cantonese food," I say. "So maybe it's good that I didn't let your mom down."

He laughs. "Maybe."

I'll let him down too. It's a sobering thought, and I lower my head.

I feel Cameron watching me. "Why didn't you come to my party?" he asks. His voice is hesitant, like he's worried about my answer.

"It's—" I'm about to tell him it's none of his business, but instead, my eyes well up, heartache stings in my chest. I don't have anyone else to tell. Nobody else cares.

"Savannah?" Cameron says, and lightly touches my arm.

I squeeze my eyes shut, trying to keep my composure. "Travis, Retha's boyfriend, OD'd. He was sent away to recover. Retha's with him." I say it all simply, trying to take the emotion out of it, but when I look at Cameron again, a tear falls on my cheek. I quickly brush it away. "He almost died," I add.

"Shit," he says. "I'm so sorry." I nod and thank him. I appreciate that his sympathy doesn't feel like pity.

"Can I take you somewhere?" he asks. He wants to help me—I know that. But I also know that he can't solve my problems.

"We can go to my house?" he offers. "We can talk there."

"I shouldn't," I say.

"Then do you want to invite me to yours?"

"*Definitely* not," I say, widening my eyes.

"Uh . . . then all signs are pointing to McDonald's. Are you hungry?"

"Not really."

Cameron exhales. "You're making this really hard."

"And what is *this*?" I look over at him. "Because in case you didn't notice, my life sucks right now." It's so confusing, liking him but knowing I can't tell him. Knowing that even if he does like me back, we can't be together. How can I have a boyfriend when I have to take care of Evan? My brother is my first priority. Not some guy. Not even Cameron.

"Yeah, I did notice," Cameron says, putting his hands in the air. "But I still want to be your friend. Why are you making it so difficult?"

"You want to be my friend?" I mean it to sound bitchy, but it doesn't come out that way. It sounds hopeful.

"Sort of. If you stop being so mean to me."

I watch him a moment, and despite my reluctance, I laugh. "That will be difficult," I say.

"I believe in you," he says. "So what do you think? Could you use a new friend?"

"No."

"You sure?"

"Okay, maybe a little," I say.

He smiles to himself and turns to look out the windshield. "So my house, then?"

"Yeah." And that's it. I suddenly have a friend, one with a fresh slate. I like it. I like the possibility. And I like him.

"I have to be home by three," I say as we walk in his front door. I slip off my shoes, proud that my socks actually match today.

"Why by three?" Cameron asks.

"Because that's when my brother's bus gets there. I can't be late." I peek around the house, half-expecting to see some remnants of a party.

"Can I meet him?" Cameron asks.

"Who?" I swing to face him. "My brother?" Evan isn't some pet that I take out for people to play with.

Cameron looks confused. "Yeah . . . I don't know. I want to meet him. Is that bad?"

"You can't meet him," I murmur, turning away. I shouldn't have come here, shouldn't have told him about Travis, because now he thinks we can share things like this. But we can't. Look what Patrick said about my brother. I can't handle that happening with Cameron.

"Hey," Cameron says, touching my shoulder. I jump, and he quickly steps back and apologizes.

This isn't going well. I know I'm being difficult, but I'm not sure how to be any other way. I watch him, unable to explain that. I don't want to disappoint him. I don't want him to disappoint me.

"Breakfast?" he asks, like he's trying to change the subject.

"No thanks."

"But it's Lucky Charms." He still looks uncomfortable, as if my not letting him meet my brother has screwed him up. "Who doesn't like Lucky Charms?"

"I don't," I say. "But knock yourself out."

"And what? You're just going to sit there?"

"Yes." I roll my eyes. "I want nothing more than to just sit there and watch."

"Wow, Savannah," he says, pushing his hands into the back pockets of his jeans. "That sounds kind of pervy."

"Oh my God. Shut up."

"What else do you like to watch?"

"I hope you drop dead." I'm laughing, embarrassed, but

also enjoying his sense of humor. He doesn't let me take myself too seriously.

"Well, then let me go put on a show for you," Cameron says, motioning toward the kitchen. I slap his shoulder and follow behind him.

We end up having Lucky Charms because he's right, who passes on Lucky Charms? Cameron eats two bowls, and we sit across the table from each other, not talking. When he finishes, he pushes his bowl away and leans back in his chair, looking at me.

"What?" I ask.

"Do you want to talk more about Retha and Travis?" he asks.

I shake my head. "I can't," I say, and immediately pause. It's too new. It hurts too much. I'll save the pain for later. Otherwise I'll fall apart right here.

"Okay," Cameron says. "What about your family? What are they like?"

"Jesus, Cameron. You ask a lot of questions."

"That's because you don't volunteer information," he says.

"Maybe you should take the hint."

He smiles, sweeping his eyes over my face. "What's your family like?" he asks again.

And for some unknown reason, I actually consider telling him. But I don't. "They're awesome."

"That's cool. Is your mom pretty?"

"What the fuck sort of question is that?"

He raises his hands in apology. "I'm just curious."

"You're always curious." I stand up, not knowing how to answer his question. I haven't seen my mother in a long time. I have no idea if she's still pretty.

Cameron takes both of our cereal bowls and brings them to the kitchen sink. He turns, leaning against the counter.

"What do you want to do now?" he asks. It's not even flirtatious. It's just a question, and I miss the dirty jokes. At least that way, we're not pretending there isn't tension.

"Is there anything fun to do here?" I ask.

"I have a pool table downstairs."

My mouth opens. "You have a pool table?"

"Yep."

"You are such a rich bastard."

"Does that mean you want to play?" he asks.

"I'll play."

He seems to like that. "Let's go, then."

Cameron walks to the staircase in the corner of the kitchen and goes down to the basement. I glance around, surprised that I can feel this comfortable here. It could be because we have something to do, but I know that it's him. He makes me feel this way.

I run my fingers through my hair, smoothing it and pretending that I belong. I descend the stairs and find Cameron already at the table, racking up the pool balls. He looks up at me.

"Does your brother have red hair?" he asks.

"No." I'm distracted by the basement—the low-hanging amber light, the old-timey vibe of it all. There's a bar, wood paneling, and a giant-ass pool table.

"You want to break?" he asks, holding out the cue to me.

I shake my head. Cameron leans over the side of the table, taking aim at the white ball. He slides the stick between his knuckles, looking outrageously hot as he concentrates. There's a loud noise when he breaks the triangle, and it startles me out of my daze.

"You're stripes," he says, walking around the table to get an angle for his next shot.

"Oh. Okay."

He takes aim. "You probably should've gone first," he says.

"Why's that?"

He makes another shot. "Because I'm pretty good."

"How do you know I'm not good?" I ask.

He flicks his gaze to mine. "You're good?" he asks like he doesn't believe it.

"I could be." I'm totally not.

Cameron misses his next shot on purpose. "Well, look at that," he says. "It's your turn, Sutton."

He walks over to my side of the table, stopping a little too close. He holds out his pool stick. Cameron's hair partially covers his eyes, and I want to brush it aside. I want to kiss him. Instead I take the cue from his hand.

"Thanks," I whisper, backing up and rounding the table.

"I can teach you how to shoot if you want," Cameron offers, following me with his eyes.

"No. I've got it." I don't even know how to play. But I try to copy the way he holds the cue between his knuckles. The stick won't stop wiggling and I miss the ball on the first try. My face warms with embarrassment.

Cameron laughs. "Here," he says, "let me just show you this one thing." He holds out his hand and I give him the cue. He models it for me. "Now you try."

I honestly wasn't paying attention. I try but can't quite get it. Cameron comes to stand behind me. He puts his hand over mine, setting the stick between my knuckles. He rests his chin on my shoulders and helps me aim. His arms feel nice around me.

We stay like this a moment too long, neither of us moving. He has to be able to feel my heart racing, or at least notice that my breathing is erratic.

"Now you hit the ball," he says softly, letting go of me and backing away.

I exhale, the stick shaking in my hand, my legs a bit weak. With as much effort as I can manage, I smack the white ball with the stick and send it soaring across the table and back, completely missing every other ball on the table. Cameron cracks up.

"Nice," he says. "I bet you hustle all the guys down at the pool hall."

"Do they even have pool halls anymore?" I ask.

Cameron shrugs. "Hell if I know."

We both smile now that the moment has passed. That intense, stomach-churning moment is gone and now I can relax. This is fine. It's okay for us to be friends like this, a little flirty. This won't hurt me. And I was right—he's the perfect distraction.

I hold up the cue, letting myself stand closer to him than normal. "Your turn, smartass," I say.

"Keep talking, Sutton." Cameron brushes his fingers against mine as he takes the stick. "You're lucky I didn't suggest strip poker."

And I am. Because I'm even worse at cards.

CHAPTER THIRTEEN

Cameron and I are waiting in front of my house, sitting in his Beamer. A couple of neighbors look as they walk by, checking out his car. But Cameron doesn't appear nervous. It's strange. If I were here with a BMW, I'd keep the doors locked.

"What time does the bus come?" he asks.

I look at the clock. "About ten minutes."

"So you probably didn't need to rush me, then?"

Earlier, Cameron had asked if he could take a nap. He even said I could join him and that it would be totally innocent. But I told him that we'd oversleep. Not that I thought we really would. But I knew that us together in his bed might involve some kissing. And kissing might involve other things, things I can't let myself feel.

I made him leave his house an hour earlier than necessary, but he's here waiting. I have no idea why he's waiting. And I have no idea why I'm letting him.

"Your mom doesn't live with you, does she?" Cameron asks.

I turn to him, feeling uneasy. "Why do you think that?"

"You haven't mentioned her. Plus . . ." He chews on the side of his lip. "You seem to be the one taking care of your brother."

I swallow hard, trying to hold his eyes, but I can't. I look out the windshield. Ashamed.

"No," I say. "My mom doesn't live here."

"Where does she live?"

My eyes sting, and I twitch my nose to keep from crying. "I don't know."

Cameron's silent for a second. Then, "What happened?"

I want to glare at him and tell him to fuck off, but I can't. Instead I feel darkness sweep over me, suffocate me, and it's hard to breathe. He's making me deal with things I want to avoid. He's making me dig in to the pain.

"One day I woke up and she was gone," I say, my voice low. "The car was gone. Clothes. Rent money. She took all of it."

"But she didn't take you," Cameron says like it's the most tragic thing he's ever heard. "Why did she leave?"

"I don't know. Maybe my dad. Maybe Evan. Me. Take your pick."

"It wasn't you."

I want to believe that. I want to believe that my mother loves me. That she just got overwhelmed but now hates herself for leaving. I used to believe that she could still come home. But she never did. And now it's too late to forgive her.

"She left me," I say. "She left Evan. We still needed her and she didn't care. I don't know if she ever did."

"I'm sorry," Cameron whispers.

"Me too."

"How long has it been?"

"Two years."

"That long?" I can hear the edge in Cameron's voice and I like it. I like that he can be angry for me. "How could she just abandon you guys?"

"It's so hard," I say, staring straight ahead and hating to admit it. "With Evan, it's really hard sometimes. There are days when I don't know what to do, and on those days, I want to run away like she did. I want to disappear." I stop. I need to shut my mouth; leaving isn't an option. "Never mind."

"What about your dad?"

"What about him?" I ask. "He started drinking after Evan was born. And then once my mom left, he got worse, kept losing his jobs. He was never Father of the Year or anything, but he wasn't always like this. We weren't always like this."

"And now?"

"Now? Now I can't stand him. He wants to give my brother away. His own son, and he wants to give him to my aunt Kathy to raise. But he can't. Evan's mine, too."

"Why would he do that?" Cameron asks.

"He says he can't handle it, but I'm the one who does it all. I do everything. And I'll keep doing it because Evan's my brother. I love him." I look at Cameron, wanting him to know me. Wanting him to know what he's getting into. "Evan is all I have."

I push my hair back from my face and watch Cameron.

The way his eyebrows pull together in concern. Like he cares about me.

"I sometimes think that if my mom would have stayed, Evan would be better," I say. "That he'd be okay. I hate her for that. I hate her for doing that to him."

"I'm sorry," Cameron says. He reaches to swipe his thumb across my cheek, letting it rest on my jaw as he holds my face. I'm crying. Damn. I'm crying in front of him. He leans toward me.

I turn away and look out the window. He was going to kiss me. I almost let him kiss me. I shouldn't have told him about my family. He isn't supposed to know things like this. I can't do this.

"Hey," Cameron whispers, but I don't look. "If your mom had a coffeepot, I'd piss in it for you."

I laugh, turning to him. "You would?"

"Absolutely."

And we stare at each other, a new comfort stretching over us. An intimacy that only sharing secrets can bring. Quiet, comfortable.

"Now that we're friends," he says, "do you want to go to a movie or something?"

"I don't go to the movies with my friends."

"No?" he asks.

"Nope."

"What do you do, then?" He looks amused, even pleased that I let him call me a friend.

"We go to 7-Eleven," I say. "Get chased by crazy bitches through a cornfield."

"I'm all for the adventure," he says. "But I thought maybe we could try something less violent. Maybe something with popcorn and armrests."

He's adorable. I straighten in the seat and look toward my house.

"I have to go," I say, not really wanting to.

"I know." Neither of us moves.

"Thanks for . . . the ride and the cereal and everything," I say.

"No problem. Thanks for letting me beat you at pool."

"You're an ass," I say. "Okay, for real this time. I'm going. I'll see you at school."

"You sure you won't come see a movie with me?"

I want to. I want to be that girl with a hot guy, sitting in a theater, eating popcorn and making out in the back row. "I can't," I say. "I have Evan tonight."

"He can come."

"No."

Cameron exhales, shaking his head. "Maybe another time, then. Have a good night, Sutton."

That's it? He isn't going to argue more? "Okay . . . bye," I say, and open the door. I feel rejected, even though I'm the one who said no. Even though I've been the one pushing him away.

I walk to my front porch and sit on the stairs, waiting for Cameron to leave. I wish I said yes to the movie.

Evan's bus turns down the street, and I jump up to meet it. I glance at Cameron, who's still waiting in his car.

As the yellow bus pulls up, Evan is in his seat, his face

pressed to the window. When the door opens, he races down the steps.

"Savannah!" he calls excitedly.

I look at the bus driver, but she shrugs, letting me know he's been keyed up the entire ride. It makes me happy, seeing him like this.

"What's up, buddy?" I ask. Comforted by his gentle touch when I take his hand.

"I made you something. It's here in my bag." He lifts his backpack, nearly tripping with his excitement.

"Thanks," I say, fixing the buttons on his jacket. I've decided not to tell him about Retha and Travis being gone. It might make him think of our mother.

"Who's that?" Evan asks, pointing toward the street.

I turn to see Cameron's BMW still at the curb. His eyes widen when I notice him, and he starts his car like he's about to take off. He's so damn curious.

"It's my friend," I tell Evan. "His name is Cameron."

"Hi, Cameron!" he yells, and waves.

Behind the windshield, Cameron's mouth opens in surprise, and then he waves back. Evan loves the attention.

"Do you want to meet him?" I ask, squatting down next to my brother, brushing his blond hair out of his eyes. He needs it cut; I'm embarrassed I let it get this long. "He has a really nice car."

"Can I ride in it?" Evan asks me, wide-eyed.

"No. But we can go look at it if you want."

Evan pulls my hand in the direction of the Beamer. Cameron rolls down the passenger window and cuts the engine.

I stagger behind Evan on the sidewalk, but he drops my hand when we get to the door and pokes his head inside the window and squeals.

"Savannah!" he yells back to me. "He has a TV in here."

I smile. He's actually talking about the GPS, but I'm not going to correct him. I walk up behind him and bend over to rest my palms on my knees. Cameron meets my eyes for a second before looking back at my brother.

"Hi, Evan," he says in a tone that isn't at all condescending. I like that. Usually when people find out Evan has a disability, they talk to him like he's stupid.

"Hi, Cameron," my brother says to him. "You have a really nice car."

"Thanks."

He's looking at my brother so completely normally that I ache inside. All I want is for people to treat my brother this way.

"Do you like video games?" Cameron asks him. Evan hangs half inside the window, pushing buttons on the dashboard.

"Yes!" Evan shouts, even though he's never played one before.

"Cool." Cameron nods. "Me too. But after I got in trouble my mom didn't let me play them anymore."

"Savannah got in trouble too," my brother says. The comment digs me—I wish Evan didn't need to know about that. At least he doesn't know why. "Can I play the video games?" Evan asks.

"Sure. You want to come over?" Cameron offers.

"Yes!"

"No," I respond at nearly the same time. Cameron takes the hint.

"Tell you what, big man," Cameron says. "I'll let you borrow my system. But you have to be really careful with it."

Evan nods frantically, and then turns to grab the bottom of my shirt. "Cameron is going to let me play his games!"

"I heard," I respond, looking into the car. "What a nice guy. I wonder why he would do something so generous." I narrow my eyes, and Cameron opens his mouth and touches his chest like he's offended that I think he has an ulterior motive.

"Because he's your friend," Evan says, shaking his head. "Friends are nice. Retha is nice."

There's a sharp pain at the mention of Retha, but I force a smile.

"Yes," I say. "Retha is nice." I look back in the car. "Cameron's sort of nice too. When he's not being a manipulative asshole."

"Hey," Cameron says. "Don't swear in front of your brother."

"Shut up," I say.

"That's not very nice either."

"Yeah," Evan says. "That's not nice, Savannah."

I resist the urge to flip Cameron off, and instead, duck inside the window.

"Are you really going to bring him video games?" I whisper. "Because he gets really fixated on things, so if you were just fucking around—"

"I'm going to bring him my Xbox. I don't use it anymore."

"Have you outgrown video games or something?" I ask.

"Hell no. By the time my mom gave it back, I already got a new system."

I shake my head. "You rich bastard." I turn to Evan and find him watching Cameron, anxious and excited. It worries me, scares me to want too much. "I don't need your charity," I say to Cameron.

"It's not charity," he replies seriously. "And it's not for you. It's for Evan."

I pause a minute, knowing Evan deserves something fun like this. I can't afford to give it to him. So I nod that it will be okay.

"Can I come by later and drop it off?" Cameron asks. His hand is lying palm up on the passenger seat, like he hopes I'll reach down and take it.

"Um . . . my dad will be here in about an hour," I say. "He doesn't let people come over."

Cameron's face softens and he brings his hand back into his lap. "What if I just drop it off?" he asks. "I won't come in or anything."

"Savannah," Evan says, holding on to the bottom of my shirt, stretching it out. "I want video games."

Cameron and I stare at each other, and there's a lot going on, but nothing being said. He's taking care of me and I'm letting him. I want to let him, even though it makes me grateful and sick at the same time.

If I could, I'd take Evan and we'd jump in Cameron's car. I'd make him drive us somewhere far away.

But I can't do that. I have nowhere to run.

I smile softly at Cameron. "I'll come outside at eight, if you want to drop it off."

He nods, then glances past me. "Hey, Evan. I'll see you around, okay?"

"Okay, Cameron. Bye!"

Evan's so happy to have met someone new. I want to hold him to me and keep the moment forever. This innocent thrill. Just us.

Cameron drives away, and Evan and I watch after him until I feel my brother's little hand slide into mine.

"He has a nice car," Evan repeats.

"Yeah," I say, looking down. "He's a good guy, too. Not like most of the assholes I bring around here, right?"

Evan shakes his head. "That's not a nice word, Savannah."

I smile. "You're right," I say, pulling him toward the house.

CHAPTER FOURTEEN

At seven thirty I put Evan to bed and clean the kitchen. I called Retha for an update, but she hasn't gotten in to see Travis yet. My father's in the living room, drinking a beer. I'm not allowed to bring people around. The only exception is Retha, and that's because she intimidates my father. Even Travis isn't allowed in the house. I slip out the back door.

Walking to the curb, I take a seat on the pavement and wait. I know there's a chance Cameron might not come back. He wouldn't be the first guy. Just because he's rich doesn't mean he wants to give charity to the poor.

I hate feeling this way.

Car lights illuminate the street, but I don't move until I know it's him. As the car slows, I see that it is. I'm happy he came back.

Cameron parks in front of me as I pull my feet off the street. He turns off the engine, and I open the passenger door and get in.

His eyes widen in surprise. "Wow," he says. "First time

I didn't have to bribe you to get into my car."

I laugh. "Not true. Video games, remember?"

"Right." He nods.

He smells good, like he's going on a date. His clothes are nice and I look shabby in comparison.

"You going out?" I ask. I'm a tiny bit jealous.

"For a little while. Why? You want to come?"

"No." It must not be a date if he's inviting me along. I know it's unreasonable for me to want him to stay single; I'm the one who keeps saying no to him. But I'm not always rational.

"There's a party," he says. "Pretty low-key."

"On a Monday?"

"It's not as cool as 7-Eleven, but it's okay."

I laugh. "Thanks, but I don't think your friends and me would mix."

He furrows his brow. "Why would you think that?"

"Are these friends all rich like you?"

Cameron looks offended by the question, and suddenly I feel like a real bitch. "Some of them are, I guess," he says. "Is that why you think they'd be assholes to you?"

"I didn't think they'd be assholes," I lie.

He watches me for a moment, looking unsure of himself. "Do I offend you?" he asks.

It catches me off guard. "No."

"Then why would you think I hung out with the sort of people who would?"

"I didn't."

"Do you want to come out to a party with me tonight, Savannah?" I can tell it's his last offer.

"No."

He swallows hard. After a second he reaches behind the seat for a canvas bag and sets it on my lap.

"It's really easy to set up," he says, avoiding my eyes. "Just a few cords. I gave him two racing games and a couple of quest games."

"Thanks. When do you want it back?" I ask.

"Whenever he gets bored of them."

"He'll never get bored of them."

"He can keep them as long as he wants." Cameron seems upset, even a little sad. I want to climb over and kiss him, tell him how much I like him. But I drop my eyes instead.

"This is really nice of you," I say. "Thank you."

"Anytime."

I feel bad because I know that Cameron thought I'd go out with him tonight, that we'd shared something and now we can be together. But there isn't enough time for him. Not when Evan is asleep in his room, needing me.

"You know I can't pay you back or anything," I say. Of course, he already knows this. I'm just stalling so I don't have to go inside.

"Your overwhelming gratitude is enough thanks for me," he says.

"Maybe I'll be nice to you now or something," I say offhandedly.

"Maybe you will."

"I can try," I murmur. I lean over, fully intending to put my mouth on his. But at the last second, I kiss his cheek instead. I close my eyes, pausing. His hand touches softly at my lower back, keeping me close. When I pull back, I keep my eyes down.

"Good night, Cameron," I whisper.

I climb out, shut the door, and begin walking to my house with the canvas bag over my shoulder.

Cameron starts the car, but before he drives away, he calls, "One of these days you'll say yes, Savannah."

"I hope so," I say to myself, and walk around to the back of my house.

Evan becomes completely obsessed with the video games. I try to hide the system from my father, putting it away before he gets home and telling Evan to keep it a secret. It's nearly impossible though—Evan can't lie. He also can't stop thinking about the game.

On Thursday night I'm about to fall asleep when I hear my father's booming voice in the living room. I curse and throw back my covers. He's probably wasted—even though he knows better than to do this when Evan's home.

"I said, where did you get it?" he shouts.

My heart seizes in my chest, and I trip over my shoes as I race out of my room. When I get out into the hallway, the house is dim except for a low light in the living room that I recognize is the TV. I can hear Evan whimpering, and I fly into a rage before I even ask what's going on.

Dad stands in front of the television, lit by the blue screen, and Evan is cowering near his feet. That fucking bastard.

"Get away from him!" I scream, ramming both of my palms into my father's chest and knocking him back a few steps. I quickly gather Evan in my arms.

"I didn't touch him," my father says with a sneer. I can smell the alcohol on him.

"But you yell at him? He's seven!" I cradle Evan in my arms, his tired tears soaking into the sleeve of my shirt.

In the light of the TV, I watch my father's eyes flick to my brother—a moment of regret, before he turns away. "Put him to bed," he says gruffly. "And then come back so I can talk to you."

"No," I say. "I have school tomorrow. I don't have time for your—"

"Put him to fucking bed, Savannah!" he yells. I recoil and tighten my arms around my brother.

I do what he asks, tucking Evan into bed and kissing his head.

"Daddy's mad at me," he whimpers. I have to bury my anger to keep him calm.

"He's not mad at you," I say. "He's mad at me. You didn't do anything wrong."

"I sneaked out to play games. I'm sorry."

"I said it's not your fault," I whisper. "Now go to sleep. You have school in the morning, and then you're going to Aunt Kathy's this weekend. Don't . . . don't tell her about this, okay?"

"Okay," he answers, and rolls over, tucking his little hand under his cheek. He's up way past his bedtime; tomorrow will be a nightmare for all of us.

My heart is pounding as I leave his room, closing the door, and return to where my father has calmed down. He sits on the couch, the light from the kitchen now on.

"I swear, if you ever—"

"Where did you get the game from?" he asks.

I stare at him, confused for a moment. "What?"

"The video game. Where did you get it? Because I sure as hell don't have that kind of money." He probably thinks I stole it.

"Retha," I lie quickly. "Her boyfriend got her a new one, so she gave me hers. I thought Evan would like it." I use Retha's name because I know my father doesn't have the balls to tell her to take it back. And he doesn't know she's in Cleveland with Travis; just in case he feels a bit brave.

My dad looks over at the system again, and then gets up to shut off the TV. "We don't take charity," he says.

What he doesn't realize is I've been taking charity every time I let Travis buy me lunch, every time Retha and her mom bring us food. No—he doesn't ask for charity. He gets to keep his pride, leaving me to sacrifice mine instead.

"It was a gift," I say, although I feel ashamed for taking it.

"Same difference," he says. He goes into the kitchen and turns off the light, leaving me alone in the living room with just the soft glow of the television.

After my father goes to bed, I call Retha, relieved when she answers.

"How is he?" I ask immediately.

"The nurse says better," she answers, sounding exhausted.

"He's awake and talking. He asked where we were."

I press my lips together, crying softly.

"He's going to make it," she says. "He's going to make it this time."

And our relief is tempered with the honesty of her statement. *This time.*

"How long before you can see him?" I ask.

"They're not saying, but I think by the end of the week, if he keeps recovering. Although it'll probably be like those supervised jail visits."

"Bake him a file cake," I say, making her laugh.

"You know I'm a shitty cook," she responds. "Now how's my little guy doing?" she asks. "Is he behaving?"

I want to tell her about what my father did tonight, how he yelled at Evan. But that would be selfish. Retha has huge problems of her own. I won't dump mine on her too. Not this time.

"He's been real good," I say. "In fact . . ." I force my voice light. "He met Cameron today."

"Whoa," Retha says. "I think you need to start from the beginning. Please tell me you're finally getting some."

I laugh, feeling better for real, and tell her about my afternoon, exaggerating where I think it'll entertain her most. When I'm done, I glance out the window and see the sun is about to rise.

"I should go," I say. "School's really going to suck. Wish you could share the misery with me."

"Oh, girl," she says. "If there's one bright side, this is it. Now go crash out for a bit. I'll give Travis your love."

I thank her, and after we hang up, I go back to my room. Talking to her has given me some footing again—settled me.

I miss her, but all I can do from here is try to make my life better before she and Travis come home.

My alarm goes off an hour later. I find some change in the bottom of the canvas bag Cameron gave us with the video games, and it's enough to take the bus to school. But by Friday afternoon, I'm out of money. Cameron has court-mandated therapy so he's not at school, making class nearly unbearable. And I have no ride home. Not to mention I kind of want to see him.

I begin walking home, thinking about Travis. I'm a few blocks away when I hear someone whistling a song behind me. I ignore it at first, but as it gets louder, I realize they're whistling for me.

I turn around.

"Hey, *Slut*ton," Patrick says. "You lost? This isn't your neighborhood."

Patrick is wearing a beanie, his hands buried in the pockets of his coat. I'm struck down with panic. What's he going to do?

When we dated, Patrick could be a jerk. He'd hurt my feelings. But he never hit me. Now things are different. He *wants* to hurt me. I can feel the hatred oozing out of his skin.

"Leave me alone," I say as if I'm not scared. But I am. He's completely unpredictable now.

"Don't be a bitch," he calls. "We just need to talk."

"Seriously, Patrick. Fuck off and die. I don't have anything to say to you."

He's approaching fast, but I can't turn my back on him. Not unless I want a boot kicking me down. I ball my hands into fists and wait. Even if I run, he'd still be able to catch me. I have to stand up to him.

Patrick pauses on the sidewalk in front of me, looking casual, almost normal. My breathing is erratic; I'm sure he can read my fear.

"Come on, Savannah," he says, smiling. "We used to have some good times, remember?"

"No."

"Aw." He laughs. "You're hurting my feelings. I used to nail you pretty good."

I feel sick. Son of a bitch.

"Then you started getting all weird," he continues, "stopped fooling around, spending all your time worried about your retard little brother. . . . Is it any wonder we broke up?"

My fingernails bite into the flesh of my hand. "You're an asshole," I say.

And before I can react, his hand darts out to grab me hard by the face, and he pulls me to him. He wraps his big arm around me, pinning my hands to my sides. He presses himself against me and brings his face close to mine, his fingers digging into my cheeks.

"Bitch," he whispers harshly, his breath thick with the smell of peppermint gum. "You need to learn some manners." I try to pull away, but he only holds me tighter. His fingers are hurting my face.

"Don't cry." Patrick leans in to lick the tear slowly off my cheek. I close my eyes at the dampness on his tongue, horrified. Vulnerable. Patrick's hand moves lower, almost on my ass.

"Stop," I choke out, but it's hard to talk with how he's holding my face.

He pulls back to grin. "Come on, baby," he says. "Just tell me you're sorry." He leans forward to brush his mouth against mine. "I bet I can make you yell my name like you used to."

I squeeze my eyes shut, wishing he were dead. I hate him. I hate him touching me. I hate his mouth near mine. "Fuck you," I say as clearly as I can.

He digs his fingers into the hollows of my cheeks until I think he might tear through my skin. I cry, I struggle, but I can't get free of his grip. I can even feel him hard against me. This is turning him on.

My tears run freely now, and all I can do is wait for whatever comes next. Because I won't apologize. I'm not sorry.

A horn beeps, startling us as a group of cheerleaders yell to Patrick from a Jetta in the street. I almost scream for help, but I know they won't help me. Not when they all wish they were the ones getting assaulted by the football king. Patrick smiles, still clutching me, still close to my face.

"We're not done," he whispers, and gives me a quick peck like I'm still his girlfriend. He pats my ass before letting go and heads over to the car of girls.

He leaves me on the sidewalk, my cheeks aching, my mouth on fire. I spit on the ground and use the wrist of my jacket to wipe his saliva off my cheek. I don't want any part of him near me.

As the car pulls away, Patrick leans out the window. "Think about what I said, Savannah." I flip him off and he laughs.

The minute he's out of sight, a deep sob tears from my chest. I put my palms on my knees and cry. I curse Patrick. I curse myself. And when I can breathe again, I walk back toward the school.

CHAPTER FIFTEEN

"How'd you get my number?" Cameron asks as I climb into the passenger seat of his car. My hands are still shaking even thirty minutes later, and I keep my head down.

"I used the school phone to call information," I say. "I wasn't sure if you were back from therapy yet. I'm sorry."

"Stop," he says. "You don't have to say—" He turns to me for the first time, and his eyes widen. "Holy shit, Savannah! What did you do to your face?"

He reaches to take my chin, turning me so he can get a better look. The gentleness of his touch is startling. I watch his eyes as he checks me over with concern.

"How'd this happen?" he asks. "You have black-and-blue marks."

I can't tell him. This is too much. He already knows about Retha and Travis, about my family; he can't know how screwed up every aspect of my life is.

"It was a Honda full of bitches," I say, trying to smile. He doesn't return it and lowers his hand.

"I don't believe you," he says.

My smile fades, and I turn toward the window. I'm humili-ated. But I had no one else to call. Kathy would have had a heart attack if I asked her to pick me up. I couldn't give her another reason to think less of me.

"Who did this to you?" Cameron asks softly.

I shake my head, refusing to say. Not wanting to admit how afraid I am.

"Was it the asshole from the truck the other day?" he asks. "Do you know him?"

But before I can answer, I burst out crying. I can still feel the slickness of Patrick's tongue on my face. His hand on my ass. The pain in my cheeks. Retha and Travis are gone and I have no one to protect me from him. He's going to kill me.

Cameron reaches over and brings me to rest against his chest as I cry. He runs his hand along my hair and he doesn't say a word. He just lets me feel and holds me until I stop shaking.

When I quiet, Cameron tucks my hair behind my ear. "Hey," he says softly. "Can we go to my house for a little while?"

I realize I'm holding on to him, my fingers knotted in his shirt. I'm becoming dependent, and I shouldn't do that to him. Not when I have so many problems.

"Just take me home," I say, sniffling and straightening up in the passenger seat. Cameron doesn't argue.

He drives me home, and when we stop at the curb, I'm surprised to see my dad's rusted truck in the driveway. He shouldn't be home yet, and dread coils up in my stomach.

"Is that your father's?" Cameron asks, looking past me at the truck.

I nod.

"I want to come inside," he says. "Will he let me?"

Cameron's bold. I turn to him and see that he's staring at me differently. Not the way he used to. Not the "whatever you say, Sutton" look. This is more intense. More expectant, like now he has something to fight for.

"He won't let you," I say quietly. I want Cameron to hold me again. I want to press my face into his neck as he strokes my hair. I want him to tell me it'll be okay—I might believe him.

"I should kidnap you," Cameron says. "Take you to my house."

"You're going to rescue me?"

"Would you let me?" he asks, nodding out the windshield. "We can go right now. There are a lot of rooms at my house. My parents won't find you for days."

I smile at him. He can't save me. He can't change my life. He's just a guy.

"Thanks for the ride, Cameron. For everything." I open the door.

"Hey," he calls. He turns his face and taps his cheek. He's playing around, but I like it. It's sweet. So I lean in and softly kiss his cheek.

I get out and walk to my house, and when I reach my door and look back, Cameron's gone.

I wish I'd left with him.

I enter my living room and find my father in the easy

chair, drinking a can of beer. His white tank top has grease smudges, and his jeans are frayed at the bottom near his boots. I keep the side of my face turned away, afraid he'll notice the bruises.

"Who was that?" he asks, his voice rumbling and drunk. He must have been looking out the window.

"A friend," I answer. "What are you doing home?"

"Is this what you do when I'm at work? Meet up with boys? Is that what you do in my house?"

I roll my eyes. "Of course not." My father acts like I do all sorts of inappropriate and terrible things when he's not around. The alcohol has made him paranoid.

"Why aren't you at work?" I ask again.

"Lost my job."

I groan. "Seriously, Dad?" I look around the room, running my hand through my hair. I suddenly notice it's gone. That bastard.

I spin toward him. "Where is it?" I yell. "Where's the Xbox?"

My father's eyes look past me, not seeing me. "Sold it."

I gasp. "You . . . sold it? It wasn't yours!"

"It wasn't yours, either, Savannah. Or Retha's. She called earlier and I asked her about it."

My heart is thumping so hard I can barely breathe. "It was for Evan," I say. I can only imagine how upset my brother will be when he gets home. He'll melt down completely.

My father takes a long sip of his beer and glares at me. "So who did it belong to?" he asks.

"It belongs to my friend. Now get it back!"

"Who did it belong to?" He raises his voice, and after everything I've been through today, it scares me. "Answer me, damn it!"

"Cameron," I say, holding up my hands. "My friend Cameron brought it for Evan, okay?"

"The one you were just in the car with?" He curses and stands up, moving toward me.

"You're drunk," I snap. I don't hang around when he's drunk—I'm not going to sit here and listen to him cry about my mother and how it's our fault that she left. For him only to forget the hateful things he said in the morning.

I bolt out of the room, and on my way to the door, I grab my father's wallet off the entry table. I pluck out a twenty-dollar bill and walk out, slamming the door behind me.

I cry my way down the street, and around Broadway I flag down a taxi. I give him Cameron's address, and the driver looks at me, his eyes lingering on my jaw—probably noticing the bruises there. But he drives anyway.

Cameron's car is in the driveway, and I'm both relieved and scared that he's home. Why would I come here? It was impulsive and stupid to just show up, but I have no money left to get anywhere else.

I pay the taxi driver, and as he leaves, I stand in the driveway and survey the house. I can't believe I ran to him again. Cameron can't help me. He can't make it all better. And yet . . . I walk up to his door, take a deep breath, and knock.

It's quiet at first, and I worry that he's not actually home. I'll be stranded, maybe still waiting in the driveway when Cameron's parents show up.

I knock again, but before I draw my hand back, the door opens.

"Savannah?" Cameron asks. He looks downright shocked to see me.

I want to apologize for bothering him. I want to leave. Instead I stand at his front door and shrug. I have nowhere else to go.

Cameron's expression softens, and he steps aside. "Come on," he says. I lower my head and walk past him.

My face is sore and my clothes feel dirty from being close to Patrick. Cameron closes the door and stands behind me.

"What else happened?" he asks.

"Where are your parents?" I ask, ignoring his question.

"They're out. Savannah . . . are you okay?"

My lip quivers, and I'm happy he's behind me so he can't see my face. "My father pawned your Xbox."

"What?" Cameron asks.

"I'd told him it was Retha's, and when he found out it wasn't, he took it and sold it."

"But it was for Evan," Cameron says angrily. "I gave it to him, not your asshole father."

"I know," I start to say, but I fall apart. Tears stream down my cheeks and I cover my face with my hands.

And he's here. Again. Cameron wraps me up in his arms, his chin resting on my shoulder as he hugs me tight. It's gentle but comforting. I don't think I've ever felt a touch like this, something so free of intentions.

"How'd you get here?" he asks.

"What do you care?"

"Just being curious again."

I laugh and step out of his arms, wiping the tears off my face before turning to him. His expression doesn't show pity; he isn't telling me how sorry he is that my life is a disaster. Because in the end, talk is just talk. I like that he knows that.

"I stole twenty bucks from my dad," I say.

"Good."

"Yeah."

He's quiet for a moment, and then leans down to slip on his sneakers. I furrow my brow, wondering what he's doing.

"Zip up your coat," he says. My heart sinks. Is he taking me home?

"I thought—"

He sighs like I'm being difficult and steps closer, taking the bottom of my jacket to zip it up. He stops, his fingers lingering near my neck, and I lift my eyes to his. He smiles and my entire body warms.

"I'm taking you out for pizza," he says.

On Friday nights, Vince's Pizza has all-you-can-eat wings. When we arrive, the lot is full and we have to park at a convenience store down the block. It's extra cold tonight, and I almost take Cameron's arm to warm up. Instead I wrap my arms around myself, and we cross under the awning to the restaurant.

"I've never been here," I say to Cameron. "Is it any good?"

Cameron scrunches his nose like he can't decide and holds open the glass door for me to enter first. I'm intimidated. The place is busy—long picnic-style tables line the room with platters of wings in the center. It's loud and rowdy in here, tons of people. I don't recognize any of them, although they seem to be about my age. The smell of pizza and wing sauce clings to everything, and it makes my mouth water.

"Two, please," Cameron tells the girl at the hostess stand, and turns to survey the room. The girl smiles widely and leans her boobs onto the stand.

"Cameron?" she says. "Holy shit—you haven't been here in forever."

He glances back at her, taking a minute to place her, and then nods. "Uh, yeah," he says. "It's been a long time."

The girl's eyes drift past him and quickly take stock of my appearance. Her mouth settles into a smile, and she grabs two menus. "Right this way," she says, and leads us through the room to a small table that's still being cleaned.

Cameron and I sit at the still-damp table, and the hostess hands us the menus and says our server will be right over.

"I used to come here a lot," Cameron says when she's gone. He runs his eyes over the menu, even though I don't think he's actually reading it.

"Guessed as much. She seemed to miss you."

He smiles and looks up, as if flattered that I'm jealous. I'm not. I mean, not really. "She was probably hoping I was here with Marcus," he says. "You're the only one trying to pick me up, Sutton."

I laugh. "You're a terrible person," I say.

A server appears at the end of the table, a guy with buzzed black hair and sauce stains on his apron. He pulls out a notepad. "What can I get you?" he asks impatiently.

He notices Cameron and holds out his hand. "Oh, shit. What's up, man?"

Cameron slaps his hand, and the two of them laugh. I keep my head down, assuming Cameron is embarrassed to be seen with me, but instead he calls my name. Terrified, I slowly look up.

"Savannah," he says, hiking his thumb at the server. "This is Reggie. We went to school together."

"Yeah, until this fucker got his ticket out," Reggie says, smiling. "Hate you, man. Captain Douchebag has been unbearable since you left. Heard they're renaming the library."

"Good," Cameron says.

Reggie says it's nice to meet me—he even sounds like he means it. As he and Cameron catch up, I glance around the room again. I watch these people and try to imagine Cameron here with them, eating pizza and wings. Playing darts. I can't help but think he doesn't fit, though. Maybe he used to.

"All right," Reggie says. "I'll be back with some wings for you guys." He slaps Cameron's hand again and leaves. When he's gone, I check out Cameron.

"Why'd you bring me here?" I ask.

"For pizza."

"You wanted to prove your friends aren't assholes," I say.

"Not true. I didn't know any of my friends would be here tonight. I haven't been back since I left school."

"Kicked out," I correct.

"Hey! What happened to you being nice to me?" he asks.

"I said that *maybe* I'd start being nice to you."

"That's right."

Reggie drops off two sodas, and as I dip my straw in and take a sip, Cameron leans his elbows on the table. He moves in closer and studies my face. "Would your friends like it here?"

The mention of my friends hits me hard in the chest. I'm not quite sure how to exist without them—don't know how to keep it together until they get back. But I have to. It's not like I have another choice.

"Yeah," I say to Cameron. "They probably would. Although Retha would get in a fight."

Cameron continues watching me. "I can get Evan another Xbox if you want," he says casually, as if I won't notice his charity. I bet he's been waiting to ask this since I got to his house.

"No," I tell him. "Besides, my dad will just sell it again."

Cameron clenches his jaw, but he doesn't push the issue. I can't let him get us another video game system, not even for my brother.

"Does your dad . . ." He pauses. "He doesn't hit you or anything, right?"

I hold his eyes. He's so concerned for me. Only Retha and Travis love me like this. Why does he?

"No." I shake my head. "I'd stab him if he did."

Cameron smiles softly. "I guess you would."

"My dad is tired," I say. "He's tired of life. He's tired of Evan. He's tired of me. He thinks that if Evan weren't born, my mom wouldn't have left."

"I'm sure he doesn't really blame him," Cameron says.

"No," I say. "He does. And when I get home tonight, he'll still be drunk."

"Then you shouldn't go home," Cameron says.

"Cool idea, but I'm not really into sleeping on park benches."

Reggie arrives at our table with a silver tray stacked high with wings. He sets it down, a few wings falling off the pile and onto the checkered plastic tablecloth. The hot sauce burns the inside of my nose in the best way and I can't stop smiling as he gives us napkins and tells us to enjoy. I can't remember the last time I had chicken wings.

Cameron's the first to grab a wing, and just as he bites down, I notice the door of the restaurant open. My smile falters and I gasp in a breath. Cameron lowers his food.

"What's wrong?" he asks, wiping his mouth.

I don't answer at first. Because Patrick is in the doorway with three of his blockhead friends, joking with the hostess. The bruises on my face begin to ache, and fear ices my skin. I saw the hatred in his eyes earlier. I can't let him hurt me again.

"We have to go," I whisper to Cameron.

"What? But the food just—"

"Please," I say, ducking down. I hate how scared I am. And I hate that Cameron will want to know why.

He stares me down, but then he nods. "Yeah, all right," he says, taking out his wallet and tossing down some cash. "But we're stopping for ice cream."

I force a smile, hoping we'll make it out before Patrick notices me. Cameron looks longingly at the wings, and then pushes back in his chair. But before he can stand, Patrick looks around from the front of the room, possibly searching for someone he knows, and his eyes come to pause on me.

The air in the room is sucked out, and I quickly lower my head.

"Is that . . . ?" I hear Patrick call loudly. He doesn't finish the sentence, but I know he's talking about me. I harden myself against him, tightening my jaw and clenching my fists below the table.

Cameron stands, but I don't move, scared to draw any more attention. I wouldn't have gotten past him anyway. Patrick walks down the aisle, glaring at me.

"Look what we've got here," he says, sounding amused. "*Slut*ton's on a date."

Cameron spins quickly to look at him, and then turns back to me, a question on his face. I want to apologize, even though I know it's not my fault. But first we have to get out of here. I start to get up, but suddenly Patrick's at the end of the table, blocking my escape.

His expression darkens. "I told you we weren't done."

"You definitely are," Cameron says, pushing past him to take my hand, pulling me out of my seat. Although Patrick is taller, Cameron's build is enough to at least give him pause. But then Patrick laughs.

"Good luck with that," Patrick says to him. "*Slut*ton—"

But he doesn't get to finish his insult because Cameron pushes him hard enough to knock him back into the table. The edge tilts, sending chicken wings and sodas to the floor. There's a smash as the cups hit, silverware clinking.

Cameron reaches down to grab Patrick up off the floor, but

Reggie comes running over and takes Cameron by the shirt.

"Ease up, man," Reggie says, holding him back. He locks his arms across Cameron's chest from behind. Another worker comes over and helps Patrick up on the other side of the table. Reggie leans in near Cameron's ear.

"Better get out of here before one of these assholes calls the police. You know how they are."

Cameron's eyes are wild, like he's ready to fight anyway, but Reggie whispers something about parole. Cameron curses, and then as if he just remembered I'm here, he glances over. He doesn't seem the least bit embarrassed that he was about to fight. Instead he laughs and holds out his hand to me.

Reggie lets him go. I take Cameron's hand and quickly lead us toward the door before Patrick and his friends regroup. I don't want to get jumped, and I certainly don't want Cameron to.

We get outside into the cold night and head toward his car. I check back to make sure no one is following us. Adrenaline races through my veins.

"You didn't have to do that," I say to Cameron when we get to the car. "We could have just left."

"That's the asshole from the truck, right?" Cameron asks. "Seems walking away wasn't enough to deter him then." He stops, and I realize that he's been holding back the true depth of his anger. "He did that to your face, didn't he?" he asks.

Shame, bright and painful, blooms across my chest. "Doesn't matter," I say, pulling up the handle of the passenger door to get in. It's locked.

"Was it him?" Cameron asks.

"Open the door."

"Just tell me."

I scoff. "Why? So you can kick his ass and go to jail? No thanks, Cameron. I don't need your fists to do the talking for me."

"They can talk for both of us," he offers.

I stare at him, and then I have to smile a little. "You're so fucking weak-willed," I tell him. "You shouldn't give in to your violent impulses."

"And he shouldn't put his hands on you." He says it seriously, deeply, like it hurts him. Yeah, well, it hurts me, too. I blink back the tears that sting my eyes.

"Technically, I stabbed him first," I say.

"He deserved it."

I wipe my nose before it starts to run, and turn away. "Didn't you promise ice cream?" I say, unable to look at him.

Cameron clicks the locks on his car, but neither of us gets in. I can feel him waiting for me, and I glance up.

"My house?" he asks. "We've got ice cream there. Even the kind with all sorts of weird shit in it, like gummy worms."

"I hate gummy worms."

"We also have chocolate."

I bite on my lip, trying to keep from smiling. I don't have to go with him. I could have him take me home.

But I don't want to be there right now. I'm still pissed at my father.

"I'll eat the weird shit," I say to Cameron, and open his car door.

CHAPTER SIXTEEN

Cameron's parents aren't home yet, so we sit at the kitchen table with a container of ice cream between us. We don't bother with the bowls.

"I meant what I said earlier," I tell him, gliding the cold spoon over my tongue. "I don't want you fighting for me. You have enough trouble."

"Fine," he says.

I stare at him. "Just 'fine'? You're not going to argue? You always argue."

He groans. "You either want me to fight or you don't." He takes a big scoop of ice cream and puts it in his mouth.

"From now on," I say, "we don't punch through our problems. Deal?"

His dark brown eyes settle on mine, and there's a hint of worry there. Stubbornness. But he lifts his spoon out like he's waiting for us to cheers on it. I clank my spoon against his, and we continue eating.

Cameron pauses, looking me over. "You should definitely stay here tonight," he says again.

"I can't stay here."

"Why not? It's not a park bench."

"What about your parents?" I ask.

"They'd be cool with it. It's not like we're getting it on or anything. We're friends. Friends can have sleepovers."

"You're an idiot."

"You want to stay here, don't you?"

"No." But I sort of do. Even if I slept on the rug in his living room, it'd be better than going back to my house.

"If my mom asks you to stay, will you say yes?" Cameron asks.

"No."

He licks his spoon, watching me with a smirk. "Okay."

Cameron lets me use a little of Kendra's makeup to cover up the bruises on my cheek. I'd hate for his parents to see them, for them to know the kind of mess I've gotten myself into.

When Kendra and Marcel get home an hour later, Cameron walks over to his mother and says something under his breath. She immediately looks at me.

"You should definitely spend the night, Savannah," she says, as if I'm arguing. "With your father out of town, I'd be more comfortable with you here."

I want to punch Cameron in the throat, but we'd already agreed to stop fighting through our problems.

"I can't stay," I tell Kendra politely.

"You can," Cameron mumbles, and goes to sit on the couch. "You just don't want to."

"That's not true," I say.

"So you'll stay?" Kendra asks.

Well, now I'll look like a huge jerk if I say no, so I press my lips into a smile and say yes. She smiles broadly and asks if we've already had dinner. Cameron and I exchange a look, not mentioning our time at Vince's Pizza, and Cameron tells her he's starving.

Kendra ends up ordering us pizza for dinner, and this time I get to eat. I don't bother calling my father to let him know where I am. I doubt he notices or even cares.

After dinner Cameron and his dad watch the end of a basketball game together, even though Cameron told me that his father was still pissed at him for vandalizing the school. When my father's pissed at me, he yells. Or he leaves. He doesn't ask me to pass the popcorn.

But whatever alternate sitcom reality I'm in, it feels safe. And I haven't felt safe in a long time.

"You sure you don't want to sleep in my room?" Cameron asks, laying blankets across the couch. "I don't mind staying out here."

Cameron's guest rooms, *plural*, are being recarpeted. And they're renovating the basement one to add another bathroom. *Another* bathroom. They already have four.

"No," I say, carrying a pillow from the linen closet. "It's your house. You get to sleep in the bed."

"But—"

"No." I turn to him, intending to be angry. But I feel

flutters instead. He's standing closer than I thought, looking all sleepy in his pajamas. Like a normal person would—only hotter. I'm wearing one of Kendra's yoga suits that is tighter than what I'd typically wear, but so soft it doesn't matter.

Cameron checks me out, and for a moment . . . I think he's going to reach for me. But he doesn't. He turns toward his bedroom instead.

"Good night, Sutton," he says. "Feel free to crawl into my bed later if you get lonely." He walks down the short hall to his room and closes the door. "Pancakes in the morning," he calls from inside.

"Great," I say back, unable to hide my smile. Alone in the living room, I sit down on the blanket and pull my knees up to wrap my arms around them. I should walk into Cameron's room right now. I think he wants me to. It would be easy.

My eyes flick to his door, and my heartbeat quickens.

"Stupid," I mumble to myself, and collapse on the couch, covering my face with my arm. I would ruin what we have. And I don't want to. This is nice. The only nice thing I have right now other than Evan.

At the thought of my brother, a sense of peace eases my heart, and I close my eyes and let myself drift off to sleep.

"Savannah." There's a voice in my ear, a shadow of movement. "Savannah."

My eyelids fly open, and Cameron is in my face. I jump and push him away, making him fall back on his ass.

"Sorry," he whispers, holding up his hands.

"What the fuck are you doing?" I ask, alarmed. I look around the room and see it's still dark.

He stares at me, confused for a second. "You . . ." He pauses. "You were calling for me."

His face is swollen with sleep, his hair messed up. "I was?" I ask.

"Yeah," he says. "Loudly. Are you okay?"

"I am. Was I just . . . yelling?"

He nods. "You were calling for me to help you. You sounded scared. I thought . . . I don't know. I thought something happened to you."

Sweat clings to my skin, the nightmare still close to the surface of my mind. The smell of Patrick's cologne is still in my nose. My cheek hurts.

I rub my palm over my face, but I can't shake him. Can't shake how he terrorized me. I squeeze my eyes shut, and when I hear Cameron get up suddenly, I see him walk into his room.

I'm disoriented, still a little frightened. Cameron comes back into the room dragging a blanket and pillow behind him.

"What are you doing?" I ask.

He throws his stuff down on the floor next to me. "Don't argue, Sutton," he says. "Just go to sleep." He gets down on the carpet and curls away from me.

"But–"

"Sleeping here," he announces.

I close my mouth with a click, staring at his back. I don't know how to thank him because no one like him has ever been willing to keep up with me this long. I want my life to be better so that I can be with him. If things were different, I'd be his girlfriend. But things aren't different. So there's no use pretending.

"How'd you sleep?" Marcel asks me at breakfast. He slides butter on his pancakes, and then reaches to grab his coffee. It's early. Too early for people to talk.

"Good," I say anyway. Cameron's across from me, eating, occasionally smiling at me. He looks really proud that he got me to stay the night.

We have to be at school in half an hour, and I'm wearing Kendra's clothes. An outfit that's still too tight, but way more stylish than anything I'd normally wear. And that includes *The Shirt*.

"Did you want any more juice, honey?" Kendra calls from where she's standing at the refrigerator. I don't know if she's talking to me, but when no one else answers, I clear my throat.

"Oh, um . . . no thanks. We have to get to school." I look at Cameron, and he curls his lip in disgust before taking a bite of his bacon.

"We could skip," he suggests.

His dad sets down his mug with a heavy thud. "What's that?" he asks. He doesn't sound amused. I wonder if he knows just how much school his son misses.

Cameron rolls his eyes. "I'm going, Dad. I was kidding."

"You'd better be," Marcel says, so intense that I feel uncomfortable. "Deal's off if you don't graduate."

Kendra leans against the counter, looking at her husband. She seems upset, obviously thinking about whatever bargain was made between her husband and son.

Cameron lowers his eyes. "Drop it, Dad."

"I will not 'drop it.' You want to waste your life? Finish high school first. That's not too much to ask."

Cameron stares down at his dish, a pink flush rising on his cheeks. His father is embarrassing him in front of me, and it sparks a bit of anger in my chest.

"I'm out of here," Cameron mumbles, pushing his chair back with a loud screech. He grabs his plate, carries it to the sink, and drops it in. We all jump at the clatter.

Cameron leaves the room and I hear the front door open and close. I'm not sure what to do. Am I supposed to chase after him? Have more juice?

"Savannah," Kendra says, startling me. "Can you make sure he gets to school okay for me?"

"Yeah," I say. But before I leave, I look at Marcel. "You shouldn't have done that when I was here. You embarrassed him." Marcel seems stunned and lowers his eyes.

Kendra walks over to take my plate and looks down at me. "Have a great day," she says. Her voice is kind, and she reaches to sweep some hair away from my face.

For a moment I want to hug her. Adults don't usually talk to me like this—act so maternal. I thank her and walk out to find Cameron.

Cameron's in his car as it idles in the driveway. I get in the passenger side, glad that it's warmed up, at least. I turn to him.

"So that was a fun family breakfast," I say. "Why's your dad so pissed?"

"Sorry about that," he says in a low voice.

"Don't be sorry. My dad pawned your Xbox, so . . ."

Cameron looks sideways at me. "Let's just say my father hasn't been as forgiving as my mother. You know, the whole hundred thousand."

"Right."

"It'll be fine. He had to pay the money, so he deserves to be angry. But if he would have just let me drop out of school, none of it would have happened."

"I don't understand," I say. "I've never wanted to drop out of school, and I stabbed somebody in math class. So why do you want to quit so badly?"

He smiles. "I want to waste my life."

"You can just leave," I suggest. "Although I'm not really sure why you'd want to."

"What. Like run away?"

"Yeah."

"No, not my style."

"Fair enough. So what's the deal your dad's talking about? What happens if you don't go to school?"

"You're awfully curious today, Sutton."

"You must be rubbing off on me. Now what kind of deal?" In truth I'm fascinated. The more I know about Cameron and how unperfect he is, the more perfect he becomes.

"My dad told me that if I didn't graduate from Brooks Academy I'd have to pay for the damages myself. I'd have to sell my car, my stuff. Then any money I have in my savings accounts. All of it gone. After that he said he'd let the state go after the rest. They'd garnish my wages. You know, if I ever got a job. But . . . I really like my car. So I agreed."

"I really like your car too," I say. "Would your dad really do that, though?"

"He would." Cameron exhales. "He definitely would."

"Then you'd better not let him find out how much school you miss."

"It'll be our secret," he whispers.

I lean my head back on the seat, watching him. "And it's not weird?" I ask. "Like, every day, it's not weird for you guys to be around each other?"

"Not really. I mean, he's my dad, right?"

I nod, but it doesn't make sense to me. At my house we wear our anger on our sleeves.

"If you're bored we could just stay in my driveway and make out," Cameron says, startling me out of my thoughts. He laughs when I look at him.

"Not this time," I say, blushing. "Besides, we'd better get you to school. I like riding around town in your Beamer. Would hate for it to get taken away."

"Glad you're thinking of my well-being."

"And you have to be close to your absent days."

"One day left," he says. "Want to cut?"

"No. I save my days in case Evan needs me."

He glances in the rearview mirror and backs out of the

driveway. When he shifts into gear, I lean over and kiss his cheek. I can't help myself. I hated seeing him look so sad and embarrassed in his house.

When I sit back in my seat, my hands trembling, Cameron's lips turn up into a grin. "You'd better be careful, Sutton," he says, watching the road. "Or you'll end up falling in love with me."

CHAPTER SEVENTEEN

With Retha and Travis gone, I don't have transportation to and from school. I'm too scared to walk, afraid Patrick will be waiting for me. I can't pretend to handle it on my own.

I don't ask, but Cameron picks me up and takes me home. I'm glad I don't have to ask, because I'm not sure I would. I love the easy way we settle into a routine. How he just seems to know what I need. And in return, all I ever give him is a simple kiss on the cheek.

After school Cameron parks in front of my house and waits with me for Evan's bus. I'd asked him not to, but he does anyway. He's very convincing with that stupid smile.

"It's Friday night," Cameron says, not looking at me.

"Awesome," I say unenthusiastically.

"Want to come out with me?"

"I can't. I have Evan tonight. Kathy has a thing." I laugh. "My aunt has more of a life than I do."

"What if you and Evan come to my house?" he says. "My mom would like to meet him."

"I can't." But when I think about it, I know that Evan would be thrilled to see Cameron's house. It might be nice to let Kendra dote on him for a little bit.

"Savannah, will you please let Evan come to dinner tonight?" he asks softly. "I'll bring you both home right after."

My chest hurts because I know that Cameron cares about me. I want to care about him, but I don't understand why he wants to get involved in something like this.

"Why?" I ask.

He looks confused. "Why what?"

"Why do you want us to come over?"

Cameron pauses, looking up the street. "I just do."

And it's such a simple answer. He doesn't profess his love or make a joke; this means more. I can feel how much he wants me there. How much he wants Evan there. I feel . . . special. My brother's bus turns onto our street.

"There's Evan," I say.

Cameron drops his head. "See you later."

"Hey," I say, slapping his thigh. "We'll come to your dinner or whatever."

He smiles, like he knew that by pouting I'd say yes. "I'll wait here."

I roll my eyes and go to wait for Evan's bus. My brother will be so excited. Meeting people always makes him happy.

"Cameron's here!" Evan yells, bolting for the car. I worry he's hoping Cameron brought a new game system to replace the one our dad sold, and when I catch up to him, he's already at Cameron's window.

"Really?" Evan says. He turns to me, wide-eyed. "He's going to take me for a ride in his car!"

"I know," I say. "Let's get you in the back and buckled up."

Evan is squealing and squirming, so I sit with him.

"I feel like a chauffeur," Cameron says as we drive toward his house.

"I wish I had one of those glass windows I could put up so I couldn't hear you," I say. Evan laughs.

"Hey," Cameron says, glancing back at him. "I thought you were on my side."

"I'm on Savannah's side."

"Thank you," I say, and wrap my arm around him.

When I meet Cameron's eyes in the mirror, he seems content. And just before I look away, he winks at me.

I'm not sure if Evan will ever want to leave. Kendra's in high gear, baking brownies and doing art projects with him. I actually watch in amazement. Her patience is really beautiful. She's better than Kathy.

"Sutton," Cameron says. I'm at the kitchen sink, and I turn to look over my shoulder at him.

"What?"

"Want to play pool?" he asks.

"No. It's getting late. We should go."

"How about a swim? My mom will let you borrow a suit."

"No. Maybe another time."

He smirks. "You actually sounded like you meant it."

"Shut up." I turn around to watch my brother a moment longer.

Evan is giggling and coloring. He's so happy, and it makes me wish he could have grown up this way. With a mother, a nice house, even a stupid pool. It's not fair that all he has is me. Okay, he has Kathy, too. But she's nothing like Kendra. My aunt cut me out of her life without waiting for an explanation. I had no one else to look after me. What sort of person does that make her? Certainly not a mother. At least, not in my eyes.

"Hey," Cameron says softly.

I sniffle. "What?"

He walks around to look at me, studying my face and seeing that I've started to cry. He doesn't mention it, but turns around and walks to the table.

"Mom," Cameron says. "I'm sorry to break up your play-date, but Evan has to go home now."

She slaps his hip. "Aw, but we're having so much fun." She turns her attention to Evan, brushing his blond hair.

"Evan," she says. He looks up at her happily. "It was very nice meeting you."

"Nice meeting you, too." But he doesn't move.

"I hope you'll come back and visit us soon," she says, not seeing it.

A wave of sickness washes over me. He's going to melt down. Right here. Right now.

"Evan," I say calmly. "It's time to go, buddy."

He turns to me, his face falling. "I don't want to go."

I dart a quick look at Cameron, but he doesn't get it either. "Evan," I say, walking toward him. "We have to go now. It's time to go home."

Evan stares at me, his crystal blue eyes welling up. "But I want to stay."

Kendra's posture changes. I kneel down in front of my brother and put my hands on his shoulders. "We have to go," I whisper.

It's almost immediate—his sobs. His violent, uncontrollable sobs. "No!" he yells.

I'm humiliated and angry with myself for putting him through this. I shouldn't have brought him here. I shouldn't have shown him this life. It isn't ours.

"Come on," I say, standing up.

He screams, sweeping the crayons off the table. I bend quickly, grabbing them and tossing them back on the table. My anger is bubbling up. Evan has to stop. To leave.

Kendra and Cameron stay out of it, and I'm glad. Most people don't. They try to comfort him or tell me how to parent him, but they only make it worse. I take a calming breath, trying to stay in control of the situation. Evan's cries and shrieks fill the room.

Marcel walks in from the living room to pause in the doorway, watching wide-eyed.

"Get up, Evan," I say, even-toned, and take his arm.

"Not. Going. To!"

So I scoop him up as he kicks at me. I pin his arms, and without a word, I carry him all the way outside and wait at Cameron's car. I hate restraining him like this. I hate other people seeing him like this. Because this isn't him. This isn't what he's about.

I hug him to me, cradling him to my chest. Wishing he

had a mom who could do this for him all the time. I whisper into his hair. "Don't cry," I say. "Please don't cry anymore."

"I want to stay," he sobs.

"Me too." I blink and lift my eyes upward. The front door closes, and Cameron walks out with his car keys, looking so sorry.

I stand by the car as Evan's cries begin to soften. Cameron meets my gaze over the roof of the car. He swallows hard and unlocks the doors.

Evan lies in my lap, alternating between shaking and whimpering. My body starts to go numb. When this happens, I have to go numb. It's too hard otherwise.

My father's truck isn't in the driveway when we pull up to the house. Thank God. I don't want to have to explain where we've been.

After he cuts the engine, Cameron gets out and comes around to open the car door for us. He reaches for Evan, but I shake my head and instead let him hold my elbow as I climb out.

I shift Evan's weight, feeling that he's fallen asleep.

"Savannah," Cameron whispers, but I can't talk right now.

"Thanks," I say, cutting off what he was going to say. "For dinner and everything."

His mouth opens like he wants to say more, but he stops and nods instead. And I knew from the beginning that letting him this close was stupid. He doesn't fit into my life. Evan needs too much from me. There's nothing left for Cameron.

I start walking toward the house, tears waiting until I can

be alone. The porch steps are steep as I try to support Evan's weight.

"Good night, Savannah," Cameron calls, sounding sad.

But I say good-bye. Because I have nothing left to give him.

Evan sleeps in my room with me. He doesn't wake up when I cry, wishing things were different. Wishing he were different, and then hating myself for the thought.

When I get up in the morning, Evan is curled up under the covers. I kiss his forehead. I close the bedroom door behind me and make my way into the kitchen.

My stomach turns.

"Where were you last night?" my father asks as he sits at the table. His clothes are ragged, and he's obviously nursing a hangover. His eyes bore into me and I look away—feeling shamed.

"Evan and I went to my friend's house for dinner." I walk over to the counter and grab the coffeepot to fill it with water.

"How nice for you," he says. "Don't you think you should have called?"

No. "You weren't here. We were home early."

I hear the scrape as he pushes his plate away. "I don't know what's wrong with you anymore," he says. "What are you doing?"

I clench my jaw and fill the coffeepot with water. "There's nothing wrong with me."

"Really? And putting a pencil through someone's hand is normal?"

"He was talking about Evan."

"I don't care, Savannah." He gets up and crosses the room, stopping at the sink and smelling like last night's booze. He watches while I put the grounds in the coffeemaker.

"He called him a retard," I whisper, wanting him to understand.

"And?" my father asks.

I turn to him, my face on fire.

He exhales. "You're not his mother." His voice softens a little. "You'll never be his mother. You can't protect him for the rest of his life."

"I sure as hell can try."

And my father looks at me. His eyes aren't angry; they're sad. "Savannah, I talked to Kathy," he says.

Oh God, no. I almost drop the can of coffee. My lip quivers as I look at him. "You didn't," I say.

He nods, his eyes welling up. I set the can on the counter, gasping for breath.

"What did you do?" I ask him, backing away. "What did you do, Dad?"

"She can give him a better life," he tries to explain. "She can be a mom to him."

"You *asshole*!" I yell, my voice cracking. "What did you do?"

"She's coming later today. I'm sorry. I don't know what else—"

But I run from him. My father has signed over custody of my brother. Of his own son. Kathy is taking Evan away from me.

I burst into my room and dive into the bed, gathering Evan up and holding him to me.

"Savannah," he whines. "I'm sleeping."

But I rock him and bite on my lip to keep my cries silent. My father has just lost everything. He's given away the only reason I have. I take care of Evan. I'm his life. He is mine. What has he done?

I kiss Evan's head and pray that we both wake up from this nightmare.

CHAPTER EIGHTEEN

My father doesn't come into my room. I figure he probably went to the living room to hate himself in private. I call Retha, but her grandmother says she went to see Travis. I have a second of relief at the fact that he can have visitors now. But when Retha's gram asks if I want to leave a message, I can't bear to say out loud that I've lost Evan. How can I ever tell anyone?

When it's almost noon, I get Evan dressed to go out. Nothing seems real. Like I'm slow walking through a nightmare.

"You want to head to the mall?" I ask my brother.

His face lights up. "Yes!" Evan loves the mall, but we rarely go. It's tough to keep an eye on him there, and we don't have money to buy anything, so it seems a bit much for a normal day. But this is our last normal day.

"Me and you, buddy," I say. "We're going to have lunch and walk around."

"And look at video games," he adds.

"Yeah," I say. I want to call Cameron, but I don't. He doesn't need to get mixed up in this now. He should be worrying about graduating, making plans for after. Meeting someone else. I close my eyes.

"Are you sad?" Evan asks, putting his palms on my cheeks.

"No," I say, smiling. "I'm just hungry. Are you hungry?"

"French fries," he announces, lifting his arms in the air.

"You got it."

I have Evan wait in my bedroom while I survey the house. Kathy may be coming to get him later, but I'm spending the day with my brother. They can all go fuck themselves. My father seems to be asleep on the couch, and I find his wallet and keys near the front door and take them.

I grab Evan by his little hand, and we weave our way quietly through the house. The door is silent when I close it.

"Where's Daddy?" Evan asks as I help him into the truck.

"He's sleeping."

"Lazy bones," Evan says, and giggles.

"Yep," I say, fixing his jacket. "Not like us, huh?"

"Nope."

And he's so happy. Not at all like the kid last night, crying and kicking. This is my Evan. And I don't want them to take him. He belongs with me.

Our dad's wallet has close to a hundred dollars in it—Xbox money. Piece of shit. I'm going to spend every cent on my brother. Every last penny.

The mall is in the middle of a renovation, but it works for us because the place is practically deserted.

The first thing I do is get Evan large fries and a strawberry milk shake. His feet swing under the food court chair as he eats. I watch him, trying to memorize every movement.

Keeping the grief buried so he won't have to see me sad.

Next we go to the pet shop, to look at the puppies and pet the rabbits. Evan squeals every time a bunny moves. It's adorable, and I actually debate buying him one. But if Kathy didn't let him keep it, it would be another reason for him to be hurt. So we settle on just watching the animals in their cages.

I buy him a truck and a stuffed animal. I buy him candy. I buy whatever he asks for, but I still want to die. I just want to die whenever I look at the clock, knowing that Kathy is waiting. My father will notice that his wallet and keys are gone. He and Kathy might call the police. Or they might just wait for me.

"I have to go to the bathroom," Evan says, holding himself.

"Don't do that," I say, pulling his hand away from the front of his pants. "I'll take you right now."

We walk quickly, finding the hallway in the construction that twists toward the bathrooms. Plastic wrap covers some of the walls, and the smell of paint is thick in the air.

There is a low whistle from behind me. When I hear it again, a pit opens in my stomach. I touch my hand to the back of Evan's head, hoping that around the corner there will be a construction worker or someone leaving the bathrooms.

I walk quickly, but when I round the corner, no one is there. Not one damn person. We're alone.

"*Slut*ton . . ."

Shit. "Come on, Evan," I say, taking the sleeve of his

jacket. I hold my breath and look back. Patrick starts to jog toward us.

I look quickly around the hall, but the only escape is the bathroom. And that would be stupid. It would be stupid to trap myself in a room with Patrick. Panic tears through my chest. Where the hell is everybody? I can't scream—it would terrify Evan. I have to get us out of this.

"*Slut*ton," Patrick sings from behind us again.

I reach the end of the hall and stop. My heart races and my fingers are trembling so badly, I'm losing my grip on Evan's jacket.

I lead Evan to the corner and kneel next to him to get on his level. "Hey, buddy," I whisper. "I have to go talk to my friend. Will you wait here?" Please don't let him hear the panic in my voice.

He stares at me for a moment, and then nods. I smile. "Sit down," I say, pointing to the floor. He slides down the wall, never taking his eyes off me.

I get up, and when I turn, Patrick is there, waiting with his big arms crossed over his chest. He leans to the side to look at Evan. "How's it going, retard?" he asks him.

My fear turns to anger, and my face catches fire. I walk straight toward him, wishing I had something to stab him with now.

"Come here," he says, taunting me. "Come here, Savannah." He opens his arms. I clench my fist, ready to punch him. I'm going to punch him until he leaves.

But before I finish cocking back my arm, there is an explosion of pain high on my left cheek where he hits me.

I stumble back, too stunned to scream. Patrick grabs me by my still raised wrist and spins me around, slamming me chest first into the tiled wall near the bathrooms.

I gasp as white-hot pain shoots up my arm, starting at my wrist and stretching up through my chest. Blood spurts on the white tile from between my lips. I try to catch my breath as Patrick holds me face-first against the wall, his heavy body leaning into me.

My face is turned in Evan's direction, forced to make him watch my expression. His eyes are wide and frightened. My wrist hurts so fucking badly, but if I cry, Evan will be so scared. He'll absolutely lose it. So I try to smile at him to let him know we'll be okay. Then I close my eyes and hold back the tears.

Patrick pushes his body further against me, pinning me to the wall and making it hard to breathe. His lips touch my ear. "You are very violent. Do you know that, Savannah?"

I keep my eyes closed. His free hand slides down over my ass, and the violation of it all nearly breaks me. I bite down hard on my lip.

"You seriously need therapy," Patrick says. His breath is hot on my ear, and I can feel that he's excited. That this sick bastard is getting off on this.

"My wrist is broken," I whisper. The cold tile on my face is good because it's keeping me from fainting. I can't open my eyes. I don't want Evan to see them.

Patrick laughs, sliding his hand between my legs. "Mm . . ." he says.

Tears leak out, running down my sore cheek. "Stop," I murmur. Helpless. So completely helpless. I whimper as he changes the grasp he has on my wrist, so that he can get closer to me. But it only makes the pain in my broken bone worse.

"You owe me an apology," he says, his tongue touching the outside of my ear.

"Please, stop . . ." This isn't happening. Patrick squeezes me hard through my jeans, and I draw in a harsh breath as I try to back up. But he uses my arm to draw me back and slam me into the wall once again, knocking the wind out of me.

"Say you're sorry," he hisses, and grips the back of my neck.

"I'm sorry," I say immediately. I want to choke on it. When I get out of here, I'm going to kill him. I'm going to drop Evan off, and then I'm going to find Patrick and kill him.

"What are you sorry for?" he prods.

I'm broken. Violated. "I'm sorry that I stabbed you, Patrick."

He makes a noise as he pushes himself against me once more, getting one last feel. He is dead. I will kill him.

"Good girl," he murmurs in my ear. "Now was that so hard?"

And suddenly he lets me go. I don't move. From the coolness on my cheeks, I know they're wet with tears. I want to collapse and sob. But I need Patrick to go first.

"Take care, Savannah," he says as if I were someone he was passing in the school hallway. "See you later, retard," he calls to my brother.

I still don't move. I want to stop shaking. I want to disappear. My face is against the tile and my arm is beginning to go numb as it hangs limply at my side. Patrick chuckles to himself before I hear his sneakers squeak along the mall floor.

When the sound is gone, I open my eyes. They're sticky with tears, and when my vision clears, I see Evan.

He's still there, where I'd told him to stay. Only he's slumped over, his hands covering his face, sobbing quietly. The front of his pants is drenched in urine, his body shaking uncontrollably. He deserves someone better than me. I can't even protect him from Patrick.

Evan deserves so much better.

I hold my arm close to my body as I shuffle over and kneel in front of Evan. I'm trembling, sick to my stomach.

"Evan," I whisper, touching his hair with my good hand. My body is trying to go into the calm I need to comfort him, but I'm struggling. I'm scared.

Evan's cries are soft, not like the meltdowns. This is something different. This is so much worse.

"Evan," I say again, hearing the catch in my voice. I can't lift him with my arm like this. "Get up," I say, strengthening my voice. "I need to leave now, Evan. Get up."

He shakes his head slowly from side to side, refusing to look at me.

"I need Cameron," I say, and it surprises me. But I swallow it down, and I say it again. "We need to get Cameron, Evan."

I don't know where else to go. I can't take him to Kathy like this. She'd never let me see him again. I straighten up, and wince as my arm accidentally bumps the wall.

"Fuck," I whisper.

"That's not nice, Savannah," Evan mumbles behind his hands.

Relief washes over me. "Buddy?" I ask. "I need you to help me. My hand got hurt and I need to go to the doctor."

"I want Cameron," he says in a low voice.

So do I. "Okay. Let's go get him. But you need to walk. I can't carry you."

And finally my brother slowly stands, keeping his face covered except for a little spot where his hands are open for him to peek through.

I start to walk, waiting for him to tag along. I'm in so much pain and I need help. The front of Evan's corduroys has turned dark where he peed them, but we have to walk through the mall to get to the truck. If I can get us to the truck, we'll be okay.

It takes a long time, but when we finally get into the parking lot, I gulp in the cool air, trying to dull my pain. Trying to forget about the aching between my legs where that bastard touched me.

It's hard to open the heavy truck door with my left hand, but I manage it. Evan climbs into the cab, and when I hoist myself in after him, pain explodes across my arm. I moan and pull the door shut. When I straighten, I catch my reflection in the rearview.

The side of my mouth is bleeding. There's a small cut on my lip where I hit the wall, and my left eye has begun to swell. I stare at myself, hating my reflection. Hating that I wasn't strong enough to fight him off. Hating that I wasn't smart enough. Fresh tears spring from my eyes, and around me, the truck reeks of urine.

I fucked up. I fucked everything up.

Evan sniffles and I look over at him as he stares out the window. I want to reach for him but my wrist is broken.

"I love you, Evan," I say instead.

"I love you, too, Savannah," he says so quietly it breaks my heart.

As best as I can manage, I start the truck and, using my left hand, slowly drive us toward Cameron's house.

CHAPTER NINETEEN

When I pull up to Cameron's house, his car is in the driveway, and I'm so grateful. I can't think right now; I can't figure out where else to go. I need help.

Evan lies listlessly across the seat and I can't lift him. I cut the truck engine, jump out, and run to the front door. I press the doorbell repeatedly.

The door swings open, and Kendra slaps her hand over her mouth when she sees me.

"Savannah?" she says, reaching out to me. I shrink away and keep my arm in front of me.

"Evan's in the truck," I say. "I . . . I can't pick him up. I'm hurt and—"

"Savannah?" Cameron's face pales when he appears behind his mother. "Christ, what's happened?"

Kendra jogs out of the house toward the truck, yanking open the passenger door to get Evan. Cameron's eyes look me over, trying to take in all my injuries.

He notices how I hold my arm.

"I'm hurt," I whisper.

He nods, licking his lips as his expression darkens. "I can see that," he says.

Kendra murmurs in Evan's ear as she carries him into the house. Watching her hold him like that makes me feel so much better. The relief is overwhelming.

I swoon.

"Savannah!" Cameron grabs me, steadying me as the world spins out of orbit. I break down.

"They're taking him away," I say, starting to cry. "They're taking him away from me."

Cameron puts his arms carefully around me, and I rest my face against his neck. I'm not sure how much longer I can stand this. Stand my life.

"Evan?" Cameron asks. "Who's taking him?"

"My father is giving him away. He's giving him to my aunt. She's coming to get him today, so I brought him to the mall—"

"Who did this to you?" Cameron asks, stroking my hair as we stand in front of his house. "Your dad?"

"My wrist is broken."

"Yeah. How'd that happen again?"

"Patrick," I murmur. "I should have just apologized to that bastard. I should have." I start to cry, letting myself because it hurts too much to hold it in anymore.

Cameron makes a sound low in his throat at Patrick's name, and rewraps himself carefully around me. He's quiet for a moment, and then he sniffles. I wonder if he's crying too. Cameron rests his cheek on the top of my head.

"I think I should take you to the hospital," he says. "You need a doctor."

"Probably."

"Hey," he whispers, leaning over to my ear. His breath is warm and comforting. "I need to get my keys from the house, okay? My mom will watch Evan so I can take you to a doctor."

But I don't want to let him go. I cling to him, and he has to reach to gently take my arm. He pulls back to look at me, bending down to meet my eyes.

"Stay right here," he says, and he's close enough to kiss me. "I need my keys." Cameron looks over my face, studying me. When I murmur okay, he runs quickly into the house.

I want to be with Evan, but I can't let him see me like this. I feel faint, and lean against the house. The pain is dulling, but my hand has swelled. I can't even bend my fingers. My eyes flutter; I need to rest for a second.

"I'm here," Cameron says, putting his arm on my back. He leads me toward the Beamer. "My mom's giving Evan a bath and washing his clothes." He helps me into the car.

I sit and stare out through the windshield, happy that Kendra will care for him while I'm gone. Guilty that I put my brother in this situation in the first place. The driver's door opens, and Cameron drops in.

He reaches over, running the back of his fingers over my bruised face. Then he leans toward me and kisses my cheek softly. I try to smile because it's nice. But I'm too tired.

Cameron starts the car, and I'm lulled by the engine. A headache starts; I might have a concussion. I close my eyes and rest back in the seat.

"Don't worry," Cameron says. "I'll take care of it," he says. "I'll take care of you."

And before I can say anything in return, I fade away.

"You're not going home tonight," Cameron says, sitting next to the bed in the hospital chair. "You guys are staying with me."

"No." I'm waiting in the sterile white room for the nurse to bring my paperwork. That asshole did break my wrist. He gave me a nice concussion, too. I hope he's dead by morning.

"Savannah?"

"I don't need your pity," I say without looking over. I'll have to work out this situation on my own. They gave me meds for the pain in my arm, but because of the concussion, it's not the good stuff. At least it takes the edge off, though.

Cameron stands, his fingers interlaced on the top of his head as he paces the room.

"You're making me dizzy," I say. "Now call your mom and see if Evan's okay."

"My mom will take care of him," he says, stopping in front of me.

"Just call her," I say, waving my hand. But even the slightest movement sends a shock of pain up my arm, and I moan.

"Hey," Cameron says. "Take a minute." I look up at him, and his bottom lip juts out. "You have a black eye," he whispers, reaching to gently run his finger under it.

His touch sends a shiver down my back. Compared to the way Patrick touched me, it's so tender. It's kindness.

My heart is broken—I'm broken. I start to shake. "He hurt me," I say. "And I couldn't stop him. I couldn't stop him, and Evan had to watch all of it." I fall apart, curling up on my side, and then crying harder because of the pain in my arm.

The bed shifts, and Cameron is next to me, his worry and misery radiating to me. He brushes back my hair where tears are making it stick to my face.

"It's going to be okay, Savannah," he whispers. "I promise."

I hate that word. Because no one can ever keep their promises—it's a lie you tell children to make them feel better. It's not going to be okay. And it will never be okay again.

"That bastard broke my wrist," I mumble into the pillow. "I hate him. I hate him so much." And I want to stab Patrick with a pencil all over again. He's taken everything from me.

"Did . . . did he hurt you anywhere else?"

I squeeze my eyes shut, trying to block out the memory. "He got his cheap feel," I say. But I'm playing it down. What Patrick did was so much worse than that. He stole my confidence, my identity.

Cameron shudders in a breath, like he's about to choke on it. He sits up, and I turn to see him wipe his face. He stands, sniffling hard, and his posture is pure anger, and I watch him slowly get it under control.

"I need to see Evan," I say.

"You can," Cameron answers, looking back at me. "But I don't want to send you home like this. Stay with me. Let Evan sleep at our house. My mom will make him pancakes in the morning—it'll be really nice for him. You need help."

He winces at the statement. "And I know you don't need me. So you have to *let* me help you."

I close my eyes. Feeling them brim over with tears. Evan loves pancakes. And ultimately, this is about him. He's all that matters.

"Okay," I say. "But I'll need to call my dad. He and Kathy might still be waiting for me. I sort of . . . took off."

Cameron's mouth opens, but he doesn't say anything. He gets out his phone and helps me dial it since I suck at using my left hand.

My father is furious. Kathy waited at the house for two hours for me and Evan, threatening to call the police if my brother isn't turned over to her tomorrow. Now she gets to make those threats.

I don't tell my dad about Patrick—he'll find a way to blame me anyway. I say that I went to the mall and slipped on some ice. I needed a cast, and now Evan and I are staying at a friend's. I refuse to tell him which one. When I hang up, I hold the phone out to Cameron.

"Take me to your house," I say, feeling small. "Just get me to Evan."

The nurse scurries into the room and helps me get through a pile of signatures. My mind seems to be fluttering in and out, drowsy and slightly disoriented.

And the feeling of cold tile is still on my cheek.

Evan is already asleep when I get back to Cameron's. Kendra had set up a fluffy air mattress in Marcel's office, covering it in pillows and warm blankets. He's curled up, his little cheeks rosy. I sit in there with him for a while, listening to him breathe in deep sleep. It's peaceful, and when Cameron comes in to get me later, I'm reluctant to leave.

"So where are you going to sleep?" I ask as Cameron folds back his sheets.

"I heard the floor's nice," he says. I climb into his bed, and Cameron pulls the blanket up to my neck, making a show of tucking in the corners.

"Seriously," I say. "Where are you sleeping?"

His eyes sweep over my face. "Do you want me to stay in here?"

"No," I answer automatically.

He nods, and I immediately regret my answer. "I'll be out on the couch," Cameron says. "Doc said to wake you up every two hours, so I'll be back."

He leans over and kisses my forehead. He's too good to me. I don't deserve it. I really don't.

Cameron crosses to the door and looks back at me before flicking off the light and walking out.

Sleep isn't easy. Every time I shut my eyes, my arm starts to ache. My mind won't shut up either. It's getting difficult to breathe, like a panic attack. They said my ribs aren't broken, but there's a deep pain in my chest. Dread. I don't want the morning to come.

"Cameron?" I call before I realize what I'm doing. It's quiet. I glance at the clock and see that it's nearly one. Everyone is probably asleep. Everyone but me.

But suddenly I don't want to be alone. Suddenly I'm terrified. "Cameron?" I repeat louder.

There's a noise outside the door, coming from the living room. Then I hear what sounds like bare feet shuffling across the wood floor. The door opens, and Cameron stands there, his eyes squinted. He isn't wearing a shirt; he looks so vulnerable.

"You okay?" His voice is raspy with sleep.

"No." I stare at him. I don't know what I want; I only know that I don't want to be alone.

Cameron moves slowly into the room, looking like he's ready to fall back asleep at any second. He stands at the edge of the bed.

"Move over," he says.

I don't immediately. Do I want him to sleep in here? I'm not sure, but I keep my cast above the blankets and slide my body farther in to where the sheets are cold. Cameron climbs in, readjusting the blankets, and curls up on his side.

"Good night," he says, meeting my eyes.

I stare at him, aching all over, lonely. Cameron blinks heavily but doesn't close his eyes. He reaches his hand out to me.

"Come here," he says.

And I don't argue. For once I don't argue with him. I move slowly, sliding over and into his arms, resting my head against his chest. His bare skin is hot against my sore cheek, but it comforts me.

"Thank you," I whisper, my eyes closing.

"Go to sleep," Cameron says, chuckling. "I'm tired."

I snuggle into him, liking the way he smells, the way he pets my hair. I listen to his heartbeat, slow and strong.

Within ten minutes Cameron's breathing deepens and

he's fallen asleep. I put my lips against his shoulder, waiting to see if he'll stir, but he doesn't.

"I love you," I murmur to him so quietly, it's barely a whisper. I pause, and when he doesn't move, I close my eyes and fall asleep in his arms.

CHAPTER TWENTY

I wake up to the sound of Evan's laughter. I smile before I open my eyes, but when I do, I'm met with an excruciating pain in my arm, chest, and face. I suck in a harsh breath as I try to sit up, which actually isn't easy with a broken wrist.

Cameron's room is filled with sunshine, the curtains pushed open. He's gone, his side of the bed empty, his door closed. My cast lies heavily on the covers, and I stare down at it. My chest and ribs ache deeply, and I pull out the fabric of my T-shirt and peer inside. Damn. There's dark purple bruising from where Patrick slammed me against the wall.

I close my eyes—just thinking his name makes me sick. The smell of him, the feeling of him near me—it crawls under my skin. I almost can't bear it. I look around the room and see Cameron's phone next to the bed. I grab it and try Retha again.

"Retha?" I say as soon as she answers. She must read the panic in my voice.

"Savvy?" she asks. "What the fuck? I've been calling you. My grandmother said you sounded upset."

"How's Travis?" I ask quickly.

"He's good," she says, and there's a soft lift in her voice. "He honestly is. They have a new program out here; counselors don't seem like total assholes, at least. Everything's going to work out," she says. "Honest."

I smile, even as my body aches. I almost don't tell her any of it.

"Savvy," she says, concerned. "What is it? What's wrong?"

Although I want to save her the worry, my control slips away.

"It's bad," I say in a low voice.

There's a rustling on the line, and I imagine she's getting out of bed. Retha has always had my back, and I know she'll have it now.

"He broke my arm, Retha," I say. "He broke my fucking arm."

There's a low growl in her voice when she asks, "Who?"

"Patrick. He found me at the mall . . . he wanted me to apologize."

"Tell me what happened. Tell me everything so I can figure out exactly how I'm going to kill him."

So I do. I tell Retha everything, even the parts I wouldn't describe for Cameron. I can still see it, still feel everything he did. It's like a horror movie starring me.

"And, Retha," I say, "he had to see it. Evan had to see it all. He pissed his pants he was so scared, and it was my fault." I cry hard, loving that I can, loving that Retha doesn't try to soothe me.

"Where are you?" she asks quietly.

"Cameron's."

She pauses. "It's six in the morning. Did you sleep there?"

"Yeah."

"Damn, girl," she says under her breath. "Now about Patrick—did the cops already pick him up?"

"I didn't call them," I say. "It'll probably be the same assholes who arrested me when I stabbed him. His word against mine—who do you think they'll believe?"

"Right," Retha says. Her voice is controlled, like that night in the cornfield. Like she's plotting something serious.

Before she can go on, my heart breaks apart. "Kathy's taking Evan, Retha. She's getting custody of him."

"No," she whispers. "Oh no."

"She's taking him today. I've lost him." The sound of Evan's laughter filters into the room, and I look toward the door, quickly wiping my tears. "Look," I tell Retha. "I can't talk about it right now. I'll call you later?"

"Of course," she says, then pauses. "I'm so sorry, Savvy."

"Love you," I say. She tells me she loves me too, and we hang up.

Just as I set the phone down, there's a knock at the door.

"Come in," I call.

The door opens, and I smile when Cameron walks in with Evan riding on his back.

"Good morning," Cameron says as if it is completely normal that I'm sleeping in his bed. "Your brother wanted to see you." He brings him to the bed and then turns around, letting him slide off.

"You're awake!" Evan calls excitedly. I hold my cast up, and Evan climbs up my body to give me a hug.

"What's that?" he says, pointing at the white plaster.

"A cast." It embarrasses me to say it, but I try to smile so he won't know that I should be ashamed. Cameron watches me, his arms folded across his chest. I hate that he saw me cry yesterday.

"Why do you have it?" Evan asks.

"I hurt my wrist."

"Your friend hurt you," my brother whispers, running his fingers over the cast.

I swallow hard.

"He isn't her friend," Cameron says, not looking at me. "Friends look out for each other."

"Like Retha?" he asks.

"Yeah. And like me." Cameron reaches to ruffle Evan's hair. "I gave you a piggyback ride, remember?"

Evan laughs. Cameron looks at me, thoughtfully, apologetically—I'm not sure. But I quickly wonder how pathetic I must look to him. In his bed, bruised, bandaged. An emotional mess.

"Your eye looks better," he says. "Are you hungry?"

I shake my head, and he scrunches up his face like he knows I'm a liar. "Evan," he calls. "Let's get Savannah some breakfast. She's being stubborn."

"Stubborn," Evan repeats, and giggles. He hops off the bed and grabs Cameron's hand, pulling him toward the kitchen.

When they're gone, I lie back against the pillows. This

should be my life. Being with my brother in a big house, eating pancakes. Why is life so damn unfair? Because by the end of the day . . . I'll have nothing left.

"Do you want me to come with you?" Cameron asks as he walks me to my dad's truck. I shake my head no. I wouldn't even have Retha do this with me. It's my nightmare—no one should have to go through it.

Evan walks behind us, carrying a bag of things Kendra gave him. Snacks, crayons, coloring books—he thinks he's so lucky. He doesn't realize that kids normally get things like this. Kids without asshole parents.

Cameron opens the door for Evan and stands with me as he climbs in. He lowers his head. "Let me come with you," he says quietly.

He's not hiding his feelings for me anymore, but I have to. We don't work. We can never work. I'm a disaster of a person.

"No," I say.

He nods, and then leans in the window toward Evan. "I'll see you around, little dude." He reaches in his fist and Evan bumps it with his; then they make them explode. Cameron must have taught him that, and it's incredibly cute.

Cameron takes a step back and turns to me. He wants to touch me, hold me, hug me. I can see it in his eyes. But he doesn't.

"Will you call me?" he asks.

"No," I say, and smile.

"So you'll just show up? Unannounced?"

"Probably."

"Okay."

He leans in, like he might kiss me good-bye. I want him to, but I sidestep him and tell Evan to buckle his seat belt. Cameron holds up his hand in a wave to both me and Evan, and then turns and walks back inside his house.

I get in the truck and let out a held breath before looking sideways at Evan. He's happy, clutching his bag of treats, excited to get home to show our dad. I can't tell him he'll be leaving with Kathy. I can't tell him that.

Kathy's dark blue minivan is in the driveway, and as I park, I find her waiting on the front porch of my house. I wonder how long she's been here. I wonder how pissed she is.

"Aunt Kathy!" Evan squeals when he sees her. I drop my eyes and turn off the engine to get out.

I walk around to Evan's door, and before I even open it, Kathy's rushing down the stairs toward us. I can only imagine how much she hates me for this.

As soon as he gets out, Evan runs to her. "Aunt Kathy," he yells. "I got pancakes."

"Hi, sweetie," she says in her quiet, patient voice. I don't want to look at her. I keep my palm on the handle of the car door, facing the street.

"And Cameron let me play pool and Kendra gave me books!"

"That's wonderful. It sounds like you had fun."

They grow quiet, but I keep my back to them, afraid to turn around.

"Savannah," Kathy says. It isn't mean, never in front of Evan, but it is a controlled anger. I take a breath and turn.

Her eyes sweep over me, her arm protectively around my brother's shoulders. And even I have to admit it looks maternal. "Are you okay?" she asks calmly.

"Yes," I lie.

"And your arm?" She nods her chin toward it.

"Broke my wrist."

"Another fight?" she asks, her face registering disgust.

"No," I say. "An accident."

She stares at me for a long moment, not believing me, but maybe not caring enough to argue. I bite on the corner of my lip, my real fear bubbling up.

"Are you going to keep him away from me?" I whisper.

She blinks rapidly, declining to answer. She looks down at Evan and he hugs her as hard as he can. He loves her. I should be happy that he loves her because he deserves that— to love someone who can take care of him. But it hurts, like a glaring light on how I've failed him.

"Evan," she says softly. "You're going to stay at my house for a while, honey. Okay?"

"Okay. Can Savannah come too?" he asks.

Kathy's lips thin. "No. She can't," she says. "Savannah has school." Evan's expression clouds, but I'm quick to reassure him.

"It's fine," I say. "Besides, I'll see you soon." It's not true, but I can't deal with truth right now. I'm not sure I'll be able to breathe once Evan is gone. I'm barely holding it together now.

Kathy meets my gaze, and there's a bit of pity in her eyes. She swallows hard and nudges Evan's shoulder. "Say good-bye to Savannah," she says quietly.

The words are a train wreck in my chest, but I fight it back. Evan comes over to stop in front of me, reaching into the small plastic bag he's been holding. "I made you a present," he says, and takes out a rolled-up paper. I worry that he senses it, that he senses this is the end. I nod toward it, unable to talk.

Evan unfolds the paper like it is a royal scroll and holds it up for me. I whimper for a second but choke it back.

It's a house. A big, beautiful, pink house.

"That's for me?" I ask, tears spilling over onto my cheeks.

"It's not white anymore," he says. "You wanted your house pink. So Kendra helped me."

"Thank you, Evan," I murmur.

He holds it out to me, and as I take it, I glance behind him at my aunt. Her stare isn't nearly as hard as I'd expected. Even she has to know how much this hurts me. Even she could appreciate that.

"Please come with me?" Evan whispers. I press my lips together to stop the quivering.

"I can't," I say, tilting my head. Not ever.

"Why?" His small voice shakes.

"I have some things to do."

"But I want to stay with you."

I brush his blond hair back from his brow. I love him so much. I love him so much this pain might kill me. "Aunt Kathy needs you to stay with her," I say. "She's a lonely old woman. She doesn't have any of her own kids to love her."

Kathy straightens in the background, but I won't regret my cruelty.

"But I want you," Evan says, and his breaths are coming out in short spurts.

"I'll come and see you."

"Who's going to make my dogs 'n' cheese?" And Evan begins to cry, covering his face.

So I break. I break all in pieces right here.

I always promised myself that I would never do that in front of him. But I give in to the desperation, the misery, the grief. I fall to my knees and grab him, holding him to me as I sob. I cry so hard that I begin hyperventilating. I bury my face in his jacket.

I can't let him go. I will die. I will die of this broken heart.

"Savannah," my aunt's voice calls softly.

But I don't look up. I want to take Evan and run. He belongs with me.

Kathy says my name again.

It takes everything I have left to pull back, my face swollen with tears. I take his hands from over his face. When he looks at me, his bottom lip juts out. He wipes the tears off my cheeks.

"Please don't cry, Savannah," he says as he hitches in a breath. "You don't cry."

I laugh, wiping under my nose. "You're right. I'm a tough bitch, huh?" He nods, but he's miserable. "Now stop making me all sappy," I tell him.

He uses both hands to clear my cheeks, erase my tears. "There," he says.

"Thank you," I whisper, knowing that I'll cry again the minute he's gone.

"We should go," Aunt Kathy says to him, glancing at me.

"I'll see you soon," I say to Evan, holding him by the shoulder. Before he can leave, I bend down. "Can I have another hug?" I ask desperately.

Without hesitation he leaps at me and squeezes me tight. It hurts my bruised chest, but I don't care. I close my eyes trying to memorize what he feels like. Come tomorrow, I'll wake up with him gone, knowing that he's no longer my responsibility. Knowing that he doesn't belong to me anymore.

"I love you," I whisper into his hair.

"I love you, too."

Holding him back, I look him over one more time and then turn to Kathy. "Can I see him tomorrow?" I ask.

She chews on her lip. "Why don't you call and we'll see?"

I nod. That's her no.

"Let's go, Evan," she says sweetly to him, taking his hand.

I watch them walk away together, and wave every time Evan turns back to me. Soon they're in the car, driving down the street.

And I stand a little longer in front of my house, dying inside.

CHAPTER TWENTY-ONE

I go inside the house, slam my bedroom door, and lie across my bed. Sobbing. Sick. Devastated.

At around five o'clock I hear my father at the front door. He must have run off so he wouldn't be here when Kathy took Evan. Bastard. He didn't even have the decency to say good-bye to his own son.

I jump up from my bed, hate burning inside me. There's no need to be civil anymore. Evan is gone.

My father is muttering to himself before he notices me standing in the hallway. He closes the door, and when he turns, he finds me glaring at him. His eyes are red, and it pisses me off. He has no right to cry over my brother. He was the one who sent him away.

"Savannah—"

"I hate you," I say in a low voice. "I should have run with him when I had the chance."

My father looks at the floor, twitching his mouth. "Maybe you should have," he says. "Or maybe you should have done like your mom and just left on your own."

"It wasn't his fault," I say. "It was never Evan's fault that Mom left."

"It wasn't his fault," he agrees. "But it was because of him."

"Don't say that! It's not true."

"It's true, Savannah," he says. "If Evan was just normal, she'd still be here. Your mother would have never left me."

"You asshole!" I yell. "It wasn't Mom who blamed Evan. It was always you, you fucking drunk. You're sick, you know," I say, shaking my head. "And she would have left you no matter what. Because she hates you as much as I do!"

In a sudden movement, my father reaches to slap me hard across the face. I stagger back, stunned, my cheek on fire. I lift my eyes to meet his, too shocked to hit him back.

In that moment, I see his rage turn to sorrow as he covers his mouth with the same hand he hit me with. His eyes are wide and apologetic.

"Don't . . ." I begin, and my voice cracks. "Don't you ever fucking touch me again."

"I'm sorry, Savannah. Please—"

I turn away, my entire body shaking. I go into my room and slam the door. I lock it, and then lean against it, trying to breathe.

He's never hit me. Resented me, belittled me, but never slapped me.

I slide down my door until I hit the carpet. I feel worthless. I feel absolutely worthless. And although I just want to pack my shit and leave, I have nowhere to go. I'm in my worst version of hell.

* * *

The phone rings well into the night. I don't get out of bed for it, and my father doesn't pick it up either. It's probably Retha; she must be worried sick. Or Cameron. But it's not Evan—Kathy would never let him call. So I don't answer.

At nine o'clock my father knocks on my door, asking if I'm going to have dinner. I tell him to drop dead. The sky outside is dark as I stand at the window, staring out. Cameron is probably thinking about me, maybe Kendra, too.

My arm aches, but I don't take any pills because I want the pain. I want to feel the pain because it's better to feel it in my arm than in my heart. And with that pain, I go to bed and go to sleep.

The morning is quiet. When I turn over, I see that school has already started. The phone rings—probably the attendance office. I never used my days, and they can't fail me unless I miss ten days. I'd saved them for Evan. I don't need them anymore. So I stay in bed.

I don't eat. The whole day goes by and I don't eat. I put my hand over my stomach where it's vibrating with hunger. I wonder how long I can go without food. My father left early in the morning, and he hasn't come back. He's probably at the bar, but I don't care.

At around dinnertime for most families, I finally walk out into the living room and pick up the phone. I dial, and my hand is shaking.

"Hello?" Kathy asks in her sweetest phone voice.

"It's Savannah," I say quietly. She's silent. "Can I see him?" I ask through the lump in my throat.

She exhales. "Not yet. He's still adjusting. It's important to be consistent, Savannah. And until he's settled, I'm afraid you'll just upset him."

I whimper. "I need to see him, Kathy."

She sniffles, and I wonder if she feels bad at all. If she feels bad for ruining my life. "This isn't about you," she says. "It's about what's best for Evan. And I know in your way, you love him. And I know he loves you. But it's too soon. It will traumatize him, Savannah. We need to do what's best for him."

"*I'm* best for him," I snap. I'm not sure I believe that's true anymore.

"Maybe in a few weeks," she says. "Call again in a few weeks, when things have calmed down."

"Don't do this," I quietly beg.

"I'm sorry. Call in a few weeks." And she hangs up.

I hold the phone to my ear, listening to the dial tone. I force myself numb and set the phone down. I walk into the kitchen and look around, not really recognizing anything. I'm a ghost in my own life.

I take a box of crackers out of the cabinet and fill a glass with water from the tap. Then I go back to my room and lock the door.

Over the next two days my father knocks only once to ask if I'm okay. I don't answer, and instead throw a sneaker at the door. Bastard.

On the third day I'm out of tears. I shower, brush my hair and my teeth. I call Retha to let her know I'm still alive. She's relieved and tells me she put the word out on Patrick. If any of our friends sees him, he'll get jumped. For people like us, I guess it's the only justice I can hope for. Right or not.

Travis is making progress in rehab, and it looks like he might get out by the beginning of summer. I told him that when he gets here, I'm taking him out for chicken wings.

I consider calling Cameron, but I wouldn't know where to start. I walk outside, squinting at the light, and sit on my front porch steps. I let the sun warm my cheeks; the black-and-blue marks have nearly faded.

A shiny black Beamer pulls up to my curb. Cameron is supposed to be in school. Not here. He cuts the engine, climbs out. I lower my eyes to the porch steps.

"Hey, Sutton," he says.

"Hi, Cameron."

I slide over on the porch step to make room for him. He sits next to me and leans forward to rest his elbows on his knees.

"How's the wrist?" he asks, nodding toward my cast.

"Itchy."

He laughs and looks back at the house. "Your shithead dad home?"

"No."

He's quiet, wringing his hands together. At first they just look red, but then I notice the bruising on his knuckles.

"Cameron," I say, pulling his arm toward me. He lets his hands hang as I take them onto my lap, checking them over. His knuckles are cut up, bruised, and swollen. It looks incredibly painful.

"What did you do?" I whisper, running my fingertip gently

over the swelling. When I look up to meet his eyes, he's staring at me.

"Someone walked into my fist," he says, not smiling.

"Both of them?"

"Yeah. Maybe some of my foot, too."

"You got in a fight?" My heart races. I want to reach out and brush his hair away from his face, beg him to take me away. Instead I let his hand go.

"I wouldn't call it a fight," he says, resting his hands in front of him again.

"Did you get arrested?" And suddenly I'm afraid. What if they take Cameron from me too?

"You sound worried, Sutton."

"I might be."

"That's sweet," he says.

"Shut up."

He laughs. "No, the police weren't involved."

I shift on the step, turning fully toward him. "Who'd you jump?" I ask.

"Don't remember his name."

"Cameron."

"Nope. That wasn't it."

I want to call him an idiot and tell him to stop being difficult, but being here with him proves how much I've missed him. Missed the way he makes me feel. It's a lot like how Retha and Travis make me feel. Like maybe I'm worth something.

I gasp as it dawns on me. "Did . . . did you hit Patrick?"

Cameron looks out at the sidewalk. "Hit. Kick. Spit on? No. I wouldn't do that."

I stare at the side of his face, warmth spreading over my chest. "You beat him up for me?" I whisper. I want to cry. It's so goddamn chivalrous.

"Beat up?" He chuckles and looks over at me. "You make it sound like I met him at the playground after school. No, Sutton. What happened is less problem solving and more revenge. In fact"—he glances at my cast—"I would say it was all revenge."

"I thought we agreed to stop fighting through our problems?" I ask.

"This was the last time—I swear." He smiles at me. "I made it count, though."

"I'm glad." And I am, because this may be the only payback I ever get. One day, maybe, I really will stop fighting. Cameron too. I want to believe that eventually we won't have to. But I also know that life isn't always fair. But we'll try our best.

"Did you get hurt?" I ask, looking him over. His face isn't bruised. It's still beautiful.

"Nope," he says. "He didn't get a chance to hit me back. And I'm pretty sure he won't bother you again. At least that's what he was saying from the pavement."

Patrick broke my wrist. His cruelty is the reason I got expelled. He's the reason Evan was taken away.

Cameron tried to make it better. And I love him for that.

We stare at each other, and I feel such loneliness, even with Cameron next to me. I want him to hold me. I want to cry, and I want him to let me and never mention it again. I motion to his hands.

"Let me see your knuckles again," I say.

"No." He grins, holding them close to him. I can tell they probably hurt.

"Let me see your stupid hands," I say.

Cameron slowly holds them out to me. "They're not stupid," he whispers, making me laugh.

But I take them again, setting them in my lap. They were injured for me, just like I would have done for Evan. I trace each of his fingers. I want to be sweet to him. He deserves to see that I can be that way.

"That feels nice," he says quietly. If I turn to him, he might kiss me. Here on the front steps of my run-down house, in my shitty ass neighborhood, this rich boy would kiss me.

Instead, with my good arm, I bring one of his battered hands to my mouth and kiss it. Just once. Then I let it go. "Thank you," I whisper.

He doesn't make it weird, and we sit quietly. Comfortably.

"Have you seen him?" Cameron asks.

I know who he means. "Not since Sunday." A pain ripples through my chest at the thought of my brother. I twitch my nose to stop the stinging in my face.

Cameron scoots a little closer so that his hip is against mine. "I'm sorry," he whispers.

I know that he is. He cares about us. He's a good person. We sit and listen to the cars pass by, and after a while I look at him.

"You're supposed to be in school," I say.

"So are you."

"I had days left."

"Yeah," he says. "This is my last one. I'll have to make it to class every time until the end of the year or they'll fail me."

I don't like the sound of that. "You need to graduate," I say.

"I know. But it's no fun without you." He smirks a little.

"I'm going back tomorrow."

"Good."

"Good."

"Can I take you somewhere?" he asks.

"Nowhere to go."

He shrugs. "My mom wants you to come over tonight."

"Your mother or you?"

"Both of us."

And I have to admit, it feels nice to be wanted. "No thanks."

"Please."

"Okay." I stand up, wiping my palm on my jeans. I don't mind going with him. There's no reason to wait here. Evan isn't coming back. I have nowhere else to be.

Cameron is still on the porch step. "Uh . . ."

"What?" I ask. "Do you still want me to?"

"Well, yeah. But I expected you to argue."

"I'm not always difficult."

"Yes, you are," he says, getting to his feet. "But I like it that way. I like when you fight me on every little goddamn thing."

I laugh. "That's why I do it. Keeping it interesting."

"I don't think you have to worry about not being interesting," he says, walking past me to the car.

"Savannah!" Kendra calls when I walk inside the house. She looks honestly happy to see me.

"Hi," I say.

"How've you been, honey?" she asks, coming over to me. "We've been so worried."

"I'm all right," I say.

Her blond hair is pulled into a ponytail at her neck, and she's dressed up, smelling like vanilla. Cameron walks into the kitchen, leaving me alone with his mother. I'm not quite sure how to act. I'm embarrassed that she knows the truth.

She presses her lips together, looking over my face. I can see that she wants to ask about Evan. "Are you hungry?" she asks instead.

"Starving," I say, making her smile.

"Oh, good," she says. "Marcel and I are going out to dinner, but I ordered two pizzas. They're in the kitchen."

My mouth opens. "You're . . . you're leaving?" One, Cameron lied to me about his mother. Two, is Kendra really okay with leaving me alone with her son? At night? After what happened to my brother, I can't believe she'd welcome me here so openly. I'm not sure how she can be so kind.

"We have reservations," she says, pulling her eyebrows together. "But if you want me to stay, we can adjust our plans."

"No," I say. "Cameron . . . you know what? Never mind."

"Sutton?" Cameron calls from the other room. His mother tsks. She probably thinks it's rude that he calls me by my last name, but I actually like when he does it. I always have.

"Have fun," I tell Kendra. She and Marcel leave, and I go into the kitchen and find Cameron with his head inside the fridge.

"You summoned me?" I ask.

"Pizza?"

"Yeah, hand me a plate."

Cameron sets two sodas on the counter, and then grabs plates for us. The moment is so normal that it stings a little going down. And I'm not sure I deserve this sort of happy, but I'm tired of fighting it.

"This is a terrible movie," Cameron says. I look sideways at him as we sit together on his leather sofa. He's sitting close. Closer than a friend would. I shift over a little.

"It's not that bad," I say. Of course his family has a huge flat-panel, only-rich-people-would-ever-waste-their-money-on-it TV.

"Terrible," he whispers.

He's right. The movie is stupid and this is stupid. We aren't even really watching it. Things are starting to get uncomfortable, both of us waiting to see if something will happen between us. It totally shouldn't because Cameron doesn't need someone like me and I shouldn't mess with someone like him. But the sexual tension is there anyway.

He clears his throat.

Shit. I should leave. Things are about to get awkward.

"Savannah?"

I don't answer.

"Hey," he says, pushing my shoulder.

I turn to him, pretending that I hadn't heard. "Oh. What?"

He smiles a little as he looks down at the couch, and then back up at me. His brown eyes search my face, pausing at my lips. "I want to kiss you so bad right now," he says.

My entire body responds, warming to him. I don't know how to answer. I'm just sort of shocked.

"Can I?" he asks.

"Kiss me?"

He laughs. "Yeah."

"No."

"Please."

"Absolutely not."

He nods, still smiling, and looks toward the TV. "Okay."

I wait a second and then I lean over, gather his T-shirt in my hand, and kiss him.

Cameron doesn't laugh or make a joke this time. Instead he kisses me hard, his tongue against mine as he pushes me back on the sofa, my legs on either side of his hips. We're both gasping, out of control like we've been waiting so long for this. Like we don't want to stop. Like we never will.

CHAPTER TWENTY-TWO

I listen to his heart, my head on his chest as we lie in his bed. I close my eyes against its steady beats. Cameron runs his fingers down my arm, stopping just above my cast and then making his way back up again. I don't want to move from here.

"Hey," he whispers into my hair.

"Don't talk," I say, but smile. "You'll ruin it."

"Right."

I fix the sheet, covering us both up, and rest my face in the crook of his neck. He's so warm, his body perfect against mine.

"Savannah," he says.

"What?"

"Thank you."

I laugh. "Uh . . . you're welcome."

"Not for that. Although that was nice." Cameron wraps me up in his arms and squeezes me. "I mean . . ." He pauses, and it's adorably awkward. "Thank you for trusting me and everything. I wasn't sure if you ever would."

There are butterflies in my stomach, and I wish I could just say what I want, but even now I can't. I lift my head and look down at him.

"I have to go home," I say.

His face falls. "Now?"

I swallow hard. "Yeah. Right now." I give him a quick peck and sit up—taking the sheet with me. I grab my clothes off the floor and get dressed. I toss the wrapper from the nightstand in the trash and watch Cameron move slowly from the bed.

When he smiles at me, that cute, inviting smile, I have to turn away. If I let him look at me that way, he'll try to convince me to stay. So I walk out and wait by the front door.

"I don't see why you had to leave so fast," Cameron says as he drives me home. "Running out on me—kind of harsh." His bruised knuckles hold the steering wheel gingerly.

"Because I don't live at your house," I say.

"You can."

"Are you going to adopt me?"

"I should."

I laugh. I can still smell his light scent on my skin, and I try to breathe it in. I crave it now. I want it. Leaning against the headrest, I watch him.

"See," he says.

"What?"

"You don't want to leave me."

"Why would you think that?"

He grins. "You may have been murmuring a few things when you didn't realize."

My face blushes. I'm not exactly sure what he is talking about, but I know it's entirely possible that I may have said something close to "I love you" at a point when I wasn't thinking clearly.

"Well," I say, straightening up. "Things said in the heat of the moment don't count."

"Who says?"

"Me."

"You didn't mean it?" he asks.

"Nope."

He smiles. "You know I feel the same way you do, right?"

"You didn't mean it either?"

He looks sideways at me, his brown eyes meeting mine. "You're lucky I know you're full of shit, otherwise that might have hurt my feelings."

But I see that I did hurt him. He turns back to the road with his jaw clenched, his eyebrows pulled together. We drive the blackened streets to my run-down neighborhood.

I don't want to hurt Cameron. Not ever. "Why do you still talk to me?" I ask. "After what you've seen, you can't possibly still want to be in my life. *I* don't even want to be in my life."

Cameron licks his lips and glances at me. "Because I love you." He says it simply, like it's just a fact. My eyes begin to water.

And I don't answer because I don't know how. I don't know how to explain how I feel about him. Don't know the words. So when he turns back to the road, I lean over and kiss his cheek. I stay there, close to him, knowing that things have changed; there's no going back. He's too important to me. There's time for him now.

Cameron looks me over, and then, with his eyes on the road, he turns his head, letting me kiss his mouth as he tries to drive. His arms draw me closer until I'm nearly in his lap.

"I'm sorry," I say softly between his lips, using my good hand to hold his cheek. "I love you," I whisper, because I do. So much. I can't lose him, too.

"I know you do," he says, kissing me with each word. "You don't have to say it because I know you do."

My tongue is in his mouth and I want him all over again, but he chuckles, moving me gently back. "You're going to make me crash, Savannah," he says. "Maybe we should just go back to my house."

I shift back into my seat, the panic fading. I have him. I don't have to fight for Cameron because I already have him. "Another time," I say. "I have to go home in case Kathy lets Evan call."

Cameron's quiet for a long moment, and then, "You're like completely obsessed with me now, aren't you?"

"Hardly."

"I love you," he says, mocking my voice.

"Shut up."

He reaches out his hand, and although I consider slapping it away, I slide my palm into his. "You didn't need to tell me," he says quietly.

"I'll remember that for next time."

"Although, it is nice to hear," he says loudly, as if I interrupted him. "Especially when you're all over me like that."

"You're needy," I say.

"I just need you. And I'm going to steal you away from all of this and never bring you back."

He's kidding, but I let myself imagine that it's true—that we both escape together. I sit quietly as Cameron holds my hand, unable to say anything else.

Retha answers on the first ring. "It's about time, bitch," she says affectionately. "I heard that Patrick got the shit kicked out of him. Who do I owe the lap dance to?"

"Cameron."

"No shit," she says. "Huh. Well, your boyfriend busted him up pretty good. Heard he got a broken leg and some stitches. Patrick told the cops he got jumped outside the 7-Eleven, but he didn't see who did it. It was in the paper this morning." She sighs. "Either way, I owe Cameron that dance."

"I'm sure Travis would appreciate that." I laugh. "How's he holding up there?"

"Great. And you know what, I don't think we've fought once since we've been here. That's got to be a record or something."

"I believe it is." I lean back on my bed and run my fingers up and down my arm, remembering the way it felt when Cameron did it. Remembering everything. "So I did it," I say to Retha, unable to stop the grin that's hurting my cheeks.

"It?" She sounds confused.

"It."

Retha is quiet, and then I hear her take in a sharp breath. "You did *it*! Was it with *him*?"

"Yep."

"Wow," she says. "I'm impressed. I mean, I knew he wanted to, but damn, girl. I didn't think he had a chance. You're not easily had. Were you wearing *The Shirt*?"

"No. I guess I don't need it anymore."

"I guess you don't," she says. "And I'm guessing it was good?"

I laugh, blushing. "Yeah, it was all kinds of good."

"I knew it."

"Now hurry home so we can go to 7-Eleven and talk about it in Travis's car," I say.

"First thing on my to-do list," she says. "But I don't want to wait. Tell me *everything* now."

I laugh, and Retha gets back to being her old self, asking for every detail of Cameron's anatomy and physiology. I don't tell her—okay, maybe I hint, but it's cool. It's cool to have my best friend, even if she can't be here with me now.

She doesn't ask about Evan, even though I know she's hoping for an update. But it's too painful right now. It's too painful for both of us. I still can't believe it's real. I can't believe he's gone.

A week goes by. Then two. I call Kathy every day, but she still says it's too soon for Evan to see me. She tells me he's good though. Happy. It shouldn't hurt to hear that, but it does. The fact that he doesn't need me.

But I still call, and Kathy promises that soon she'll let me come by. Legally I have no rights to Evan—my father had been telling the truth; she had a good case for custody. Kathy's not his mother, but she's not my mother either. She's better.

CHAPTER TWENTY-THREE

"Your aunt seems reasonable," Kendra says as I sit at the kitchen table on Thursday. "So maybe she's just taking the advice of a well-meaning therapist. I'm sure she'll let you see him soon."

Cameron and Marcel are picking up takeout, and Kendra is using the opportunity to ask about Evan. She's been waiting for a while.

I look at her, trying to see if she thinks my aunt is better for Evan than me. But I don't see that kind of judgment in her eyes.

"You're a good person, Savannah," she says softly. "I'm sure Kathy knows how much you love him."

And my heart aches because in all my life, no one has ever said that I'm good. I've been badass, I've been beautiful, and I've been a bitch. But I've never been good. I look down at the table.

"I miss him," I whisper as my face begins to tingle with the beginnings of a cry.

"I know you do," she says, brushing my hair back from my shoulder. "And you've been so brave. You really have."

Cameron is lucky to have had her his whole life. And I'm lucky because Kendra lets me stay at their house whenever I want. I want to every night, but I do it only on the weekends. I don't want to be a burden.

"How are things with your father?" she asks, taking a sip of her iced tea.

"Okay." Things are awful. After he slapped me, I refused to speak to him. Even when he gets drunk and yells my name from the living room, sometimes crying, I don't answer him. I can't. He gave Evan away. He just gave him away, and I'll never forgive him.

Kendra watches me for a moment, probably knowing that I'm lying, but she just nods. The front door opens and Cameron's laugh travels in from the entryway. Kendra and I look at each other, and she smiles.

"Hey," Cameron says to me as he walks in the room.

"Hi."

He sets a plastic bag with trays of food on the table and comes to put his hands on my shoulders.

"What'd you get to eat?" I ask, looking up at Cameron. "And please don't say Cantonese."

"Of course," he says. "It's your favorite." He leans down and pecks my lips. "I'm just kidding. It's spaghetti with extra meatballs."

"You guys need anything before we leave?" Kendra asks us, taking out two plates for us.

"Nope," Cameron says, pulling out a chair to sit next to me. "But I think you should ask Savannah to stay over. She always says no when I ask her."

I turn to glare at him, but he only smiles.

"Honey," Kendra says to me. "Please stay the night. I don't like the idea of you being alone. Cameron says your father is never home."

For a second I want to be defensive. I want to be mad at Cameron for talking about me when I'm not around, but I know it's because he cares. Not because he doesn't.

"I'll stay tonight," I say, but drop my eyes. I'm still embarrassed of where I came from.

"I'm glad," Kendra says. "I like when you're here. It's nice to have another girl around."

I thank her and watch as she leaves the room. When she's gone, Cameron shifts in his chair, putting his elbows on the table.

"Sorry," he says from next to me.

"It's okay."

He grabs my chair and pulls it until it's up against his. Cameron wraps his arms around me and puts his chin on my shoulder. I love when he does that. He always seems to know when I need it.

"You really shouldn't talk about me when I'm not here," I say, mostly joking.

"I can't help that I worry about you. My mom worries too."

I lean my head away to look at him, raising my eyebrows.

He's telling the truth. I can see it in the softness of his brown eyes, the way he watches me.

"You shouldn't worry," I say.

He laughs. "Uh, yeah. I totally should."

"Stop." My wrist still itches under my cast. I can't even think about the mall without the fear of a panic attack.

"I'll try," he says.

"Great."

He waits a moment. "So you want to go watch bad movies and sleep in my room with me?" He bites playfully at my shoulder.

I push him back, making him laugh. "And sure, let's watch your stupid movies."

"Oh, now they're stupid?"

"Shut up."

"I love when you sleep in my room with me," he says, leaning in again. Despite wanting to be tough, I kiss him.

It should be weird that I sleep in his room, but his parents don't mind. They don't even ask us to leave the door open. Not that we have sex when they're home or anything, but still . . . that amount of trust? It's sort of weird and cool at the same time.

So after his parents go out, and we watch a movie—we're in his bed. He lies next to me, twisting my hair between his fingers as I stare at his ceiling.

"Then what about August?" he asks. "Can we go then?"

"No."

"But you're not going to college."

"Hey," I say, elbowing him. He chuckles, pulling me

to him. "I'm not saying it's a bad thing. I'm not going either."

"Yeah," I say, smiling. "But you're sort of dumb, remember?"

"Right. I forgot."

Cameron's going to finish the semester with an A despite having missed ten days this quarter. He should have probably lost a letter grade for that, but Mr. Jimenez saw that he was trying. He ended up being a pretty awesome teacher.

"Besides . . . I might take a class," I say, a little self-consciously. For my career project, I'd researched how to become a special education teacher. Retha looked up nursing, and we both decided that if we ever went to college, that's who we'd be. Of course, back then it was hypothetical. I had Evan.

"Ah, I snagged myself a college girl," Cameron says. "Fine. We'll go between semesters. We'll just drive. Stop whenever."

"Sounds horrible."

"Hey," he says. "Be nice."

I lift my head to look at his face. His strong jaw. His perfect lips, smirking as he stares up at the ceiling. "Look at me," I whisper.

His eyes glance over to mine, studying my face. "I always look at you," he says. "You just don't always notice."

Everything about him. I love everything about him. I move up to kiss softly at his lips, and he holds me close. We take our time. There's no rush.

"This weekend," he says after. "You want to try to see Evan?"

"Yeah. I'll call." And I feel the emptiness again. The sense of loss that never goes away. I grow quiet, and Cameron buries his face in my hair.

"It's okay to miss him," he says.

So I do. I miss my brother, and I decide that I won't make Cameron take me home anymore. Because without Evan there . . . it's not really home.

CHAPTER TWENTY-FOUR

My graduation gown is incredibly itchy. Cameron and I stand in line, waiting to enter the auditorium. Brooks students are allowed to graduate with the public school, and the entire production is way over-the-top.

Mr. Jimenez is up front, giving us instruction on how to walk out, but none of us are paying attention to him. When we start in, I notice two people standing in the doorway. My heart jumps, and I hear Cameron's breath catch in front of me.

I step out of line, and Cameron asks if I want him to wait. I tell him I'll meet him inside. He squeezes my hand and heads in with the group.

I walk to the doorway, my eyes brimming over with tears. He's here. Although Kathy made me wait to see him, she brought Evan here. And it means everything.

I kneel down on the dirty hallway and open my arms. Evan comes running. He jumps all over me, knocking me on my ass and smothering my cheeks with kisses. I eventually get him settled enough to hug him, and then hold him back so I can get a look at him.

"You're so tall," I tell him, wiping under my eyes as I cry off the makeup Kendra helped me put on. Evan's hair is cut short, and his clothes are new and clean. He looks like a regular little boy, even though I know he's so much more.

"I made you this," Evan says, holding out a necklace. It's not macaroni but actual beads. It's beautiful, and I let him slip it over my head. The necklace reaches right to my heart.

"Savannah," Kathy says, stepping up. She helps Evan up off the floor, and I pull myself back together, trying to look like a responsible adult so she won't regret letting me see him.

Evan stays at her side instead of mine. It hurts, it really hurts . . . but if he's happy, that's all that matters.

"I love you," I mouth to him. He beams in return.

Kathy holds out an envelope to me. "I got you something," she says. She keeps her eyes down, almost regretful. At first I think it's my fault, but then I recognize it's guilt. She knows how she's hurt me. She might even be sorry.

I take the card, and she tells me to open it. There's a check for several hundred dollars, and I quickly look over at her. I open my mouth to tell her it's too much, but she holds up her hand to stop me.

"It's for all the birthdays and holidays I missed," she says, and then smiles gently. "It's for all you did for Evan." She steps closer and reaches to put her hand on my arm. "I'm proud of you, Savannah," she says. "I'm really proud of you."

I can't respond. Inside, I have a million feelings at once, but more than anything . . . she's *proud* of me. She's finally proud of me.

I nod and sniffle hard, looking away. I can't even say thank you, afraid I'll start crying. She seems to understand and backs up to take Evan's hand.

"You'd better get inside," she says, wiping her eyes. She laughs. "You wouldn't want to miss the ceremony after all this."

I start toward the door. Kathy calls my name again.

"Would you . . . would you want to come over for dinner this weekend?" she asks. "I'm sure Evan would like to show you his room."

"Yes!" Evan says, wide-eyed. "I got a new bed, Savvy! It's big!"

"I'd love to see it," I tell him. I look at Kathy, barely able to catch my breath. "Thank you," I tell her, meaning it more than I ever have. I open the door of the auditorium; a voice on the microphone is welcoming people. Before I walk in, I turn to look at my aunt.

"Is it okay if my boyfriend Cameron comes to dinner?" I ask. I can't believe I just called him that.

"Cameron's a good friend," Evan announces, tugging on Kathy's hand.

"Sure, I'd love that," she tells me.

I smile and blow Evan a kiss. And then I walk into the auditorium to graduate from high school.

"Congratulations, Savannah," Mr. Jimenez says as I meet him in the center of the stage. The past few months have worn him down—he's sprouting a few gray hairs. But he's a good man, and I hope he gets a better gig next year.

"Thank you," I say, taking the diploma from his hands. I'll actually miss that class full of delinquents.

"Smile!" Kendra yells from the crowd. She and Marcel have made a big deal out of all of this. They're treating it more like a sporting event than a graduation. I half expect them to be waving around one of those giant foam fingers.

I look out with an embarrassed smile, waiting for the flash of her camera. I can't hurry off the stage fast enough, hating to be the center of attention. When I get back to my seat, the folding chair is cold even through my graduation gown.

I lean to the side. "You look really sweet in that hat," I say to Cameron. His blond hair pokes out as he regards me with a mocking stare.

"Thanks, Sutton," he says. "And that was a pretty nice smile you flashed up there. Can't wait to frame it."

I laugh. "Shut up."

Cameron pats my leg and motions to the audience. "By the way," he says quietly, "little man looked real good back there."

"Yeah" I say. "He did. Oh, by the way, Kathy asked if I'd come over for dinner this weekend. I told her you'd come too."

He turns to me, realizing the gravity of the request. "She did?" he asks. I nod, and he smiles to himself. "Cool. Yeah, I'll go. I'll be all charming and shit. Can't wait to hang out with Evan. I've got a new handshake I want to teach him."

I smile, staring at the gymnasium floor. "He'll like that," I say.

My father doesn't come to the ceremony. I thought I

wouldn't care, but I do. In a way, I wish he'd shown up sober. But this is reality. And in reality, he's probably home, drinking and hating me. But mostly hating himself.

I'm doing my best to accept that he'll never be my dad again. Accept that my mother's gone forever. I pretend it doesn't hurt most days, but it does. But I've finally learned to stop blaming myself. The past few months have shown me that I have to let go to live. It isn't my fault that I couldn't make a normal family for Evan. I shouldn't have had to.

Cameron leans in and whispers in my ear. "Congratulations, Savannah."

I close my eyes, his breath so warm and comforting. "You know how I feel, right?" I say, turning to him. "I don't have to say it or anything, do I?"

"Nope," he says, putting his arm around me. "You don't have to say it."

"Good."

"Good."

Cameron pulls me closer to him, his lips against my temple. "But if you want to tell me anyway, you can."

"You're so needy."

"Tell me." I pull back and look over, loving how he continues to watch the stage and not me. He taps his finger against his cheek.

I can't help it. I lean over and kiss him, completely helpless but in a different way. "I love you." I say it so quietly, there's no way he could have heard me.

"So obsessed with me," he says.

I laugh, and his eyes glance into mine, happy, satisfied.

"I love you, too, Savannah," he says. "And now I think we should take that road trip. Explore the world being all lovey-dovey and shit."

"No."

"Please."

"Absolutely not."

He waits. Then, "We'll leave next weekend."

"Sounds good."

He squeezes me, laughing in my hair. "We'll stop at Disney and get Evan some mouse ears."

"He'll love those."

"We'll get Retha some too."

"No," I say. "She'd want something more sparkly."

"Right."

"And we'll get Travis the Goofy hat," I say. "He'll be home by then."

It's not guaranteed that Travis will be let out of rehab that soon, but Retha believes it. So does Travis. I talked to him on the phone last night and sent him my love. He sounded good. And he didn't make any promises.

Sometimes it's hard. You can care so much about a person, give so much . . . but I've learned that love isn't always enough. Still, we believe in Travis's recovery, we count on it, we go on like it *will* happen—a definite. We don't dwell on the alternative.

I look at Cameron, studying his face before softly kissing his lips. A raucous applause startles me, and around us the auditorium gets to its feet, clapping wildly.

I stand and look over the crowded auditorium, trying to

find Evan. When I find him, my face immediately tingles. He see me too and starts waving, calling out to me.

"I love you, buddy," I say, although he can't hear me.

Aunt Kathy meets my eyes and smiles. She doesn't hate me. She might even actually love me. Or at least she wants to. And I'm trying to be a better person. Someone Evan can look up to. I wave to Kathy and turn around.

When I sit, Cameron takes my good hand and holds it. He doesn't look at me, but he still sees me. He's always seen me.

For the first time, I'm filled with hope. For Evan. For me. And for the future I never thought I deserved.

ENTER THE TERRIFYING WORLD
OF THE PROGRAM IN SUZANNE YOUNG'S
NEW YORK TIMES BESTSELLING SERIES. . . .

TURN THE PAGE FOR A GLIMPSE OF BOOK 1!

THE AIR IN THE ROOM TASTES STERILE. THE LINGERING scent of bleach is mixing with the fresh white paint on the walls, and I wish my teacher would open the window to let in a breeze. But we're on the third floor so the pane is sealed shut— just in case anyone gets the urge to jump.

I'm still staring at the paper on my desk when Kendra Phillips turns around in her seat, looking me over with her purple contacts. "You're not done yet?"

I glance past her to make sure Mrs. Portman is distracted at the front of the room, and then I smile. "It's far too early in the morning to properly psychoanalyze myself," I whisper. "I'd almost rather learn about science."

"Maybe a coffee spiked with QuikDeath would help you focus on the pain."

My expression falters; just the mention of the poison enough to send my heart racing. I hold Kendra's empty stare—a deadness behind it that even purple contacts can't disguise. Her eyes are ringed with heavy circles from lack of sleep, and her face has thinned sharply. She's exactly the kind of person who can get me in trouble, and yet I can't look away.

I've known Kendra for years, but we're not really friends, especially now. Not when she's been acting depressed for close to a month. I try to avoid her, but today there's something desperate about her that I can't ignore. Something about the way her body seems to tremble even though she's sitting still.

"God, don't look so serious," she says, lifting one bony shoulder. "I'm just kidding, Sloane. Oh, and hey," she adds as if just remembering the real reason she turned to me in the first place. "Guess who I saw last night at the Wellness Center? Lacey Klamath."

She leans forward as she tells me, but I'm struck silent. I had no idea that Lacey was back.

Just then the door opens with a loud click. I glance toward the front of the classroom and freeze, my breath catching in my throat. The day has just become significantly worse.

Two handlers with crisp white jackets and comb-smoothed hair stand in the doorway, their expressionless faces traveling over us as they seek someone out. When they start forward, I begin to wilt.

Kendra spins around in her seat, her back rigid and straight.

"Not me," she murmurs, her hands clasped tightly in front of her like she's praying. "Please, not me."

From her podium, Mrs. Portman begins her lesson as if there's no interruption. As if people in white coats *should* be waltzing in during her speech on the kinetic theory of matter. It's the second time the handlers have interrupted class this week.

The men separate to opposite sides of the classroom, their shoes tapping on the linoleum floor as they come closer. I look away, opting to watch the leaves fall from the trees outside the window instead. It's October, but the summer has bled into fall, bathing us all in unexpected Oregon sunshine. I wish I could be anywhere else right now.

The footsteps stop, but I don't acknowledge them. I can smell the handlers near me—antiseptic, like rubbing alcohol and Band-Aids. I don't dare move.

"Kendra Phillips," a voice says gently. "Can you please come with us?"

I hold back the sound that's trying to escape from behind my lips, a combination of relief and sympathy. I refuse to look at Kendra, terrified that the handlers will notice me. *Please don't notice me.*

"No," Kendra says to them, her voice choked off. "I'm not sick."

"Ms. Phillips," the voice says again, and this time I have to look. The dark-haired handler leans to take Kendra by the elbow, guiding her from the chair. Kendra immediately lashes out, yanking her arm from his grasp as she tries to clamor over her desk.

Both men descend on her as Kendra thrashes and screams. She's barely five feet, but she's fighting hard—harder than the others. I feel the tension rolling off the rest of the class, all of us hoping for a quick resolution. Hoping that we'll make it another day without getting flagged.

"I'm not sick!" Kendra yells, breaking from their hold once again.

Mrs. Portman finally stops her lesson as she looks on with a pained expression. The calm she tries to exude is fraying at the edges. Next to me a girl starts crying and I want to tell her to shut up, but I don't want to attract attention. She'll have to fend for herself.

The dark-haired handler wraps his arms around Kendra's waist, lifting her off the floor as she kicks her legs out. A string of obscenities tears from her mouth as saliva leaks from the corners. Her face is red and wild, and all at once I think she's sicker than we ever imagined. That the real Kendra is no longer in there, and maybe hasn't been since her sister died.

My eyes well up at the thought, but I push it down. Down deep where I can keep all my feelings until later when there's no one watching me.

The handler puts his palm over Kendra's mouth, muffling her sounds as he whispers soothing things into her ear, continuing to work her bucking body toward the door. The other handler dashes ahead to hold it open.

Just then the man holding Kendra screams out and drops her, shaking his hand as if she bit him. Kendra jumps up to run and the handler lunges for her, his closed fist connecting with her face. The shot sends her into Mrs. Portman's podium before knocking her to the ground. The teacher gasps as Kendra flops in front of her, but Mrs. Portman only backs away.

Kendra's top lip is split wide open and leaking blood all over her gray sweater and the white floor. She barely has time to process what happened when the handler grabs her by the ankle and begins to drag her—caveman style—toward the exit. Kendra screams and begs. She tries to hold on to anything within her reach, but instead she's leaving a trail of blood along the floor.

When they finally get to the doorway, she raises her purple eyes in my direction, reaching out a reddened hand to me. "Sloane!" she screams. And I stop breathing.

The handler pauses, glancing over his shoulder at me. I've never seen him here before today, but something about the way he's watching me now makes my skin crawl, and I look down.

I don't lift my head again until I hear the door shut. Kendra's shouts are promptly cut off in the hallway, and I wonder momentarily if she was Tasered or injected with a sedative. Either way, I'm glad it's over.

Around the room, there are several sniffles, but it's mostly silent. Blood still covers the front of the room in streaks of crimson.

"Sloane?" the teacher asks, startling me. "I haven't gotten

your daily assessment yet." Mrs. Portman starts toward the closet where she keeps the bucket and mop, and other than the high lilt of her voice, she has no noticeable reaction to Kendra being dragged from our class.

I swallow hard and apologize, moving to take my pencil from my backpack. As my teacher sloshes the bleach on the floor, choking us with the smell once again, I begin to shade in the appropriate ovals.

In the past day have you felt lonely or overwhelmed?

I stare down at the bright white paper, the same one that waits at our desk every morning. I want to crumple it into a ball and throw it across the room, scream for people to acknowledge what just happened to Kendra. Instead I take a deep breath and answer.

NO.

This isn't true—we all feel lonely and overwhelmed. Sometimes I'm not sure there's another way to feel. But I know the routine. I know what a wrong answer can do. Next question.

I fill in the rest of the ovals, pausing when I get to the last one, just like I do every time. *Has anyone close to you ever committed suicide?*

YES.

Marking that answer day after day nearly destroys me. But it's the one question where I have to tell the truth. Because they already know the answer.

After signing my name at the bottom, I grab my paper with a shaky hand and walk up to Mrs. Portman's desk, standing in the wet area where Kendra's blood used to be. I try not to look down as I wait for my teacher to put away the cleaning products.

"Sorry," I tell her again when she comes to take the sheet from me. I notice a small smudge of blood on her pale pink shirtsleeve, but don't mention it.

She looks over my answers, and then nods, filing the paper in the attendance folder. I hurry back to my seat, listening to the tense silence. I wait for the sound of the door, the approaching footsteps. But after a long minute, my teacher clears her throat and goes back to her lesson on friction. Relieved, I close my eyes.

Teen suicide was declared a national epidemic—killing one in three teens—nearly four years ago. It always existed before that, but seemingly overnight handfuls of my peers were jumping off buildings, slitting their wrists—most without any known reason. Strangely enough, the rate of incidence among adults stayed about the same, adding to the mystery.

When the deaths first started increasing, there were all sorts of rumors. From defective childhood vaccines to pesticides in our food—people grasped for any excuse. The leading view says that the oversupply of antidepressants changed the chemical makeup of our generation, making us more susceptible to depression.

I don't know what I believe anymore, and really, I try not to think about it. But the psychologists say that suicide is a *behavioral contagion*. It's the old adage "If all your friends jumped off a bridge, would you, too?" Apparently the answer is yes.

To fight the outbreak, our school district implemented the pilot run of The Program—a new philosophy in prevention. Among the five schools, students are monitored for changes in mood or behavior, flagged if a threat is determined. Anyone exhibiting suicidal tendencies is no longer referred to a psychologist. Instead, the handlers are called.

And then they come and take you.

Kendra Phillips will be gone for at least six weeks—six weeks spent in a facility where The Program will mess with her mind, take her memories. She'll be force-fed pills and therapy until she doesn't even know who she is anymore. After that they'll ship her off to a small private school until graduation. A school designated for other returners, other empty souls.

Like Lacey.

My phone vibrates in my pocket and I let out a held breath. I don't have to check to know what it means—James wants to meet. It's the push I need to get through the rest of the period, the fact that he's waiting for me. The fact that he's *always* waiting for me.

As we file out of the classroom forty minutes later, I notice the dark-haired handler in the hallway, watching us. He seems to take extra time on me, but I try hard not to notice. Instead I keep my head down and walk quickly toward the gymnasium to find James.

I check over my shoulder to make sure no one is following me before turning down the stark white corridor with the metal double doors. It's nearly impossible to trust anyone not to report you for suspicious behavior. Not even our parents—especially not our parents.

It was Lacey's father who called The Program to tell them that she was unwell. So now James, Miller, and I do everything we can to keep up the front at home. Smiles and small talk equal well-balanced and healthy. I wouldn't dare show my parents anything else. Not now.

But once I turn eighteen, The Program loses its hold on me. I won't be a minor so they can no longer force me into treatment. Although my risk doesn't technically lower, The Program is bound to the laws of the land. I'll be an adult, and as an adult it's my God-given right to off myself if I so please.

Unless the epidemic gets worse. Then who knows what they'll do.

When I get to the gymnasium doors, I push on the cold metal bar and slip inside. It's been years since this part of the building was used. The Program cut athletics immediately after taking over, claiming it added too much competitive stress to our fragile student population. Now this space is used for storage—unused desks piled in the corner, stacks of unneeded textbooks.

"Anyone see you?"

I jump and look at James as he stands in the cramped space underneath the folded bleachers. Our space. The emotionless armor I've been wearing weakens.

"No," I whisper. James holds out his hand to me and I meet

him in the shadows, pressing myself close to him. "It's not a good day," I murmur against his mouth.

"It rarely is."

James and I have been together for over two years—since I was fifteen. But I've known him my entire life. He'd been best friends with my brother, Brady, before he killed himself.

I choke on the memory, like I'm drowning in it. I pull from James and bang the back of my head on the corner of the wooden bleacher above us. Wincing, I touch my scalp, but don't cry. I wouldn't dare cry at school.

"Let me see," James says, reaching to rub his fingers over the spot. "You were probably protected by all this hair." He grins and lets his hand glide into my dark curls, resting it protectively on the back of my neck. When I don't return his smile, he pulls me closer. "Come here," he whispers, sounding exhausted as he puts his arms around me.

I hug him, letting the images of Brady fade from my head, along with the picture of Lacey being dragged from her house by handlers. I slide my hand under the sleeve of James's T-shirt and onto his bicep where his tattoos are.

The Program makes us anonymous, strips us of our right to mourn—because if we do, we can get flagged for appearing depressed. So James has found another way. On his right arm he's keeping a list in permanent ink of those we've lost. Starting with Brady.

"I'm having bad thoughts," I tell him.

"Then stop thinking," he says simply.

"They took Kendra last period. It was horrible. And Lacey—"

"Stop thinking," James says again, a little more forcefully.

I look up at him, the heaviness still in my chest as I meet his eyes. It's hard to tell in the shadows, but James's eyes are light blue, the sort of crystal blue that can make anyone stop with just a glance. He's stunning that way.

"Kiss me instead," he murmurs. I lean forward to press my lips to his, letting him have me in a way that only he can. A moment filled with sadness and hope. A bond of secrets and promises of forever.

It's been two years since my brother died. Practically overnight, our lives were changed. We don't know why Brady killed himself, why he abandoned us. But then again, no one knows what's causing the epidemic—not even The Program.

Above us the bell for class rings, but neither James nor I react. Instead James's tongue touches mine and he pulls me closer, deepening our kiss. Although dating is allowed, we try to keep our relationship low-key at school, at least when we can. The Program claims that forming healthy bonds keeps us emotionally strong, but then again, if it all goes horribly wrong, they can just make us forget. The Program can erase anything.

"I swiped my dad's car keys," James whispers between my lips. "What do you say we go skinny-dipping in the river after school?"

"How about you get naked and I'll just watch?"

"Works for me."

I laugh, and James gives me one more squeeze before taking his arms from around me. He pretends to fix my hair, really just messing it up more. "Better get to class," he says finally. "And tell Miller he's invited to watch me swim naked too."

I back away, first kissing my fingers and then holding them up in a wave. James smiles.

He always knows what to say to me. How to make me feel normal. I'm pretty sure I wouldn't have survived Brady's death without him. If fact, I know I wouldn't have.

After all, suicide is contagious.

SUZANNE YOUNG is the *New York Times* bestselling author of the Program series. Originally from Utica, New York, Suzanne moved to Arizona to pursue her dream of not freezing to death. She is a novelist and an English teacher, but not always in that order. Suzanne is the author of *The Program*, *The Treatment*, *The Remedy*, *The Epidemic*, *Hotel for the Lost*, and *A Need So Beautiful*.

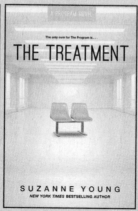

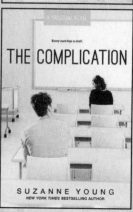